GETTYSBURG

CLASSICS OF
CIVIL WAR
FICTION

(p. 13)

A BATTLE IS TO BE FOUGHT HERE

GETTYSBURG

*Stories of Memory,
Grief, and Greatness*

ELSIE SINGMASTER

Introduction by Lesley J. Gordon

THE UNIVERSITY OF ALABAMA PRESS
Tuscaloosa and London

*Published in Cooperation with
the United States Civil War Center*

First paperback edition
Copyright © 2003
The University of Alabama Press
Tuscaloosa, Alabama 35487-0380
All rights reserved
Manufactured in the United States of America

Originally published in 1907 by Charles Scribner's
Sons. Published 1913 by Houghton Mifflin Compa-
ny. Some of the stories first appeared in *Harper's,
Lippincott's, McClure's,* and *Scribner's* magazines.

∞
The paper on which this book is printed meets the
minimum requirements of American National Stan-
dard for Information Science–Permanence of Paper for
Printed Library Materials, ANSI Z39.48-1984.

Library of Congress Cataloging-in-Publication Data

Singmaster, Elsie, 1879–1958.
    Gettysburg: stories of memory, grief, and
    greatness / Elsie Singmaster; introduction by
    Lesley J. Gordon.— 1st pbk. ed.
        p. cm. — (Classics of Civil War fiction)
    "Published in cooperation with the United
State Civil War Center."
    ISBN 0-8173-1279-X (pbk. alk. paper)
    1. War stories, American. 2. Gettysburg, Battle
of, Getysburg, Pa., 1863—Fiction. 3. Pennsylva-
nia—History—Civil War, 1861–1865—Fiction. I.
United States Civil War Center. II. Title. III.
Series.

    PS3537.I867 G4 2003
    823'.52—dc21   2002028696

British Library Cataloguing-in-Publication Data
available

1863-1913

FOUR SCORE and seven years ago our fathers brought forth on this continent, a new nation, conceived in Liberty, and dedicated to the proposition that all men are created equal.

Now we are engaged in a great civil war, testing whether that nation, or any nation so conceived and so dedicated, can long endure. We are met on a great battle-field of that war. We have come to dedicate a portion of that field, as a final resting place for those who here gave their lives that that nation might live. It is altogether fitting and proper that we should do this.

But in a larger sense, we cannot dedicate — we cannot consecrate —we cannot hallow — this ground. The brave men, living and dead, who struggled here, have consecrated it, far above our poor power to add or detract. The world will little note, nor long remember what we say here, but it can never forget what they did here. It is for us, the living, rather, to be dedicated here to the unfinished work which they who fought here have thus far so nobly advanced. It is rather for us to be here dedicated to the great task remaining before us — that from these honored dead we take increased devotion to that cause for which they gave the last full measure of devotion — that we here highly resolve that these dead shall not have died in vain — that this nation, under God, shall have a new birth of freedom — and that government of the people, by the people, for the people, shall not perish from the earth.

ABRAHAM LINCOLN.

GETTYSBURG, NOVEMBER 19, 1863.

CONTENTS

ILLUSTRATIONS

INTRODUCTION

LESLEY J. GORDON

E LSIE Singmaster published thirty-eight books and nearly three hundred short stories during a writing career that spanned more than forty years. At the height of her popularity, Singmaster gained wide readership for her ability to interweave a personal knowledge of the Pennsylvania Dutch country with dramatic characterization. She wrote for both adults and juveniles, creating realistic and entertaining narratives that thrilled her sizable audience. Two of her novels, *Basil Everman* (1921) and *Bennett Malin* (1922) gained critical acclaim for their skill and polish. Today, few have heard of Singmaster, much less know her work. But as readers will find in this republished collection, her writings continue to have as much resonance and meaning today as they did decades earlier.[1]

Singmaster was born in Schuylkill Haven, Pennsylvania, in 1879, the only daughter of John Alden Singmaster and Caroline Hoops. Although her mother was a descendent of English Quakers, Elsie was profoundly influenced by her father's German and Lutheran roots. After studying writing at Cornell University, she completed her Bachelor of Arts degree at Radcliffe College, graduating Phi Beta Kappa in 1907. In 1912, she married musician Harold Lewars, but after the deaths of both her husband and their infant son, Elsie settled in Gettysburg where her father served as president of the Lutheran Theological Seminary. She would remain in the college town until her death in 1958.[2]

Had Singmaster been male, she probably would have followed her father's example and entered the clergy. But her gender limited her options, and after the tragic end to her marriage and motherhood, she devoted herself to a

literary career. Singmaster began story-
telling at an early age and writing pro-
fessionally when she was twenty-six.
Pious, socially active, witty, and out-
spokenly patriotic, Singmaster represented a new generation of women
coming of age at the turn of the century. Though on the surface she
seemed to fit the ideal of the nurturing
and refined Christian Victorian woman,
she also had a strong feminist streak.
She was a successful author who never
remarried and stayed childless until
her death. When Gettysburg College
sought to exclude women from admis-
sions in the early 1930s, Singmaster led
the charge against the ban. She angrily
attacked the college, giving public
addresses, writing letters, and publish-
ing an article in protest. "She was a
determined tiger," one friend recalled,
"fearless when she thought she was
right."[3]

Most of Singmaster's fiction and non-
fiction centered on her Christian faith
and eastern Pennsylvania roots. She
wrote about native Pennsylvanian

Thaddeus Stevens, the Susquehanna River, and the German immigrants of her home state. But it was the Civil War and the battle of Gettysburg that in particular intrigued Singmaster, and she returned repeatedly to these topics.[4]

Gettysburg is a collection of nine separate stories, introducing readers to a wide spectrum of characters, all touched in some way by the battle. Readers will find men and women, soldiers and civilians, each offering different perspectives of the experience, ranging in dates from the first day of fight to the author's own time.

Many of the main characters are residents of the town, and two women, Mary Bowman and Hannah Casey, appear in three separate selections. In "July the First" Bowman is a young soldier's wife and mother shocked into realizing that the war has actually come home to her quiet community. "The Battle-Ground" changes the scene to November 1863 when Abraham Lincoln visited Gettysburg to give his famous address to commemorate the national cemetery. By this time, four months after the battle, Mary is distraught and distracted, her clothes still stained with blood from tending the wounded. She is oblivious to her two young children as she frantically keeps searching for her missing husband's body. The image of this gaunt, determined woman looking for shallow mass graves, convinced that she must find her husband's remains, is unforgettable. Only Lincoln's words, meant to comfort the nation, comforted the widow, enabling her to find the strength to accept her husband's death and move forward. In "Mary Bowman" Singmaster returns readers to the Bowman household one last time. It is the fiftieth anniversary of the battle, and the aging widow, now a grandmother, rarely talks about the battle and gains no pleasure in recalling the past. Relying on her religious faith, she simply awaits the next world: "she has great hope; as her waiting has been long, so may the joy of her reunion be full."[5]

Hannah Casey, in contrast to the staid and quiet Mary Bowman, is an Irish immigrant, stereotypically "burly," flamboyant, superstitious, and gullible.[6] She is pathetic and simple-minded, prattling "incessantly enthusiastically, with insane invention" of the gory battle.[7] Paired with the grieving Mary Bowman, Hannah Casey perhaps is meant to provide some comic relief. Instead, she only underscores the widow's grief and suffering.

Other stories explore issues of bravery, loyalty, memory, and war's wastefulness. "The Home-Coming" tells the story of a frightened young federal soldier named Parsons who finds himself on the eve of battle in his hometown. "Victory" is based on the actual wartime experiences of Frank Haskell, an aide to General John Gibbon. "Gunner Criswell" moves ahead to 1910 to the commemoration of a Union regimental monument when a blind veteran comes back to the battlefield, only to discover that his name is inadvertently left off the memorial. "The Substitute" champions the significance of the men in the ranks over that of the higher-ups and commissioned officers. "The Retreat" and "The Great Day," both deal with memory and the troubling irreverence expressed by some toward those who actually witnessed the battle and its aftermath.

Perhaps the strongest theme in this collection is the painful and lasting ways in which the battle affected individuals. Most of Singmaster's key characters, Mary Bowman, soldier Parsons, Frank Haskell, Gunner Criswell, "Old Man Daggett" in "The Substitute," "Grandfather Myers" in "the Retreat" and Billy Gude in "The Great Day," all seem to bear scars from the violence and its after effects. Some, like the widowed Mary Bowman and Gunner Criswell appear to find some peace, although the pain and sadness linger. Others, such as Parsons, Haskell, and Grandfather, die with issues unresolved, their individual identities lost. Substitute Daggett and Billy Gude seem frozen in the past, unable or unwilling to separate themselves from the battle's brutality and somberness.

Several of the plot lines and settings clearly replicate Singmaster's own life and influences: Although some of the characters' names seem to be of German descent, none of the characters speaks with an obvious accent. Several characters have happy childhoods but difficult and painful adulthoods. Mary Bowman in particular is perhaps closest to the author's own self. Bowman, like Singmaster, is an innocent young mother and wife when her musician-husband dies tragically. After much soul-searching, Bowman finds some strength and consolation in the words of Lincoln and in her own Christian faith. Gunner Criswell too is similarly young and happily married when a battle wound steals his sight and his young wife suddenly dies. He, like Bowman, and perhaps Singmaster, finds comfort in events outside and larger than oneself. As much as Singmaster celebrates the individual in these stories, she stresses their ties to something bigger, something even more important, lasting, and profound than their own selves. Here we see the convergence of the author's Christian faith, eastern Pennsylvanian roots, and sense of history.

Singmaster's collection was just one example of the voluminous literature produced to commemorate the battle of Gettysburg's semi-centennial anniversary in 1913. Other writers, including veterans themselves, sought to capture in words what had happened on those hallowed fields some five decades prior. These writers and their many readers wanted a personal connection to that past, whether real or vicariously. Americans realized by 1913 that something historic had occurred during the 1860s, and they wanted to remember and publicly commemorate it.

Much of this desire to remember the past was a reaction to the present. By 1913, the United States was undergoing dizzying change due to the ongoing effects of the Industrial Revolution, immigration, and the onset of modernism. The United States was fast becoming a world power with economic and political interests extending beyond its boundaries. It was a perplexing and confusing time for many, but white native-born Americans in particular began to look wistfully back to the Civil War and even to the antebellum era, believing it was a simpler and more innocent time. The Civil War became a great morality play in which it was clear who the "winners" and "losers" were.

But in fact, public memory of the war was reconfiguring who were the winners and who were the losers. Confederates were no longer defeated rebels; they, like the victorious Federals, were proud Americans who simply believed strongly in their "cause" and fought to defend it. Slavery, its cruelties, complex implications, and consequences were forgotten, as were black Americans in general. It was a white story of courageous Federals and brave Confederates.[8]

Elsie Singmaster's *Gettysburg* is very much part of this sanitized memory of the Civil War. Although her collection emphasizes the cruelty of war and its painful effects on individuals, there is no mention of slavery or black Americans. Only once does a black character, a "colored porter" in the "Substitute," appear in her collection. Singmaster's silence on the issue of slavery and the status of black Americans is perhaps not surprising but no less disquieting. She, like many white Americans, wanted to forget this part of our national history. White Americans did not want to remember the realities and cruelties of slavery and the racist ideology that allowed it to exist and thrive for three centuries. In fact, the racism that underpinned slavery persisted well into the twentieth century. The status of southern blacks was little different from what they faced as slaves.

Nor do Confederates appear in *Gettysburg* as rebels seeking to destroy the

Union. Instead, Singmaster depicts white southerners as fellow countrymen; they are not faceless, heartless foes, but brave adversaries. In "Victory" she asks her readers: "Is this conquered foe a stranger, will he now withdraw to a distant country?" "He is our brother," she answers, "his ills are ours, these wounds which we have given, we shall feel ourselves for fifty years."[9]

When *Gettysburg* first appeared, it gained great popular and critical acclaim. One critic commended Singmaster's ability to "strike the note of reality on every page." For readers who had only "lived their lives in the midst of peace," he wrote, these stories provided "some notion of the 'red harvest and the aftermath' of war."[10] Another reviewer claimed that Singmaster had grown up in Gettysburg (she actually moved there when she was an adult) and thus "unconsciously absorbed Gettysburg's local color." He added that she created characters with the "ring of sincerity and truth."[11] Her "series of vivid pictures of the great battle . . . all have a ring of genuine sympathy and sincerity," read another review.[12] A critic for *The Nation* stated: "Miss Singmaster has lived in Gettysburg for many years without that disillusion which so often comes to the dweller at a shrine."[13] Singmaster seemed to strike the right tone with her many readers in 1913; sentimentality mixed with the appropriate amount of authenticity and candor.

Readers today will equally find Singmaster's stories memorable and insightful. Her tales tell us as much about the battle and its real effects on individuals, as it does about the times in which Singmaster herself lived. Her writing also provides deep insight into war in a much broader sense. By masterfully using the metaphor of an innocent town, terribly traumatized and changed permanently, she addresses broadly war's effect on society. In the last pages of *Gettysburg,* she describes the "excess of tenderness for these dead, yet mixed with it is a strange feeling of remoteness. We mourn them, praise them, laud them, but we cannot understand them." "To this generation," Singmaster wrote in 1913, "war is strange, its sacrifices are uncomprehended, incomprehensible."[14]

Nearly seventy years after Singmaster wrote those words, Americans still strive to understand the Civil War, its causes and its consequences. Yet, despite more than a century of wars, and a new era of terrorism and fear, many Americans continue to view the Civil War in a romantic light. Civil War reenactors and buffs enjoy recounting minute details of battles, especially Gettysburg, focusing on tactics and grand strategies, famous generals and courageous soldiers, trying to recapture what they believe was the grandeur of the times. But the reality of this war, as Singmaster so dramatically depicts, scarred combatants and civilians alike. It was hardly as glorious as it now seems. The Civil War, like all wars, was gory, messy, and chaotic. Its effects were not entirely admirable, and its legacy remains contested. Works like Elsie Singmaster's *Gettysburg* are vital to understanding this.

Notes

1. Jayne K. Kribbs, "Elsie Singmaster," *Dictionary of Literary Biography: American Novelists, 1910–1945,* vol. 9, pt. 3 (Detroit, Mich.: Gale Research Company, 1981): 32–36.

2. Biographical information from Susan Hill, "Elsie Singmaster," in *Witness at the Crossroads: Gettysburg Lutheran Seminary Servants in the Public Life,* ed. Frederick K. Wentz (Gettysburg: Lutheran Theological Seminary at Gettysburg, 2001); and Susan Colestock Hill, "Seeking Fruitfulness: The Life of Elsie Singmaster, Victorian Woman in Ministry" (master's thesis, Lutheran Theological Seminary at Gettysburg, 1999).

3. Quoted in Hill, "Elsie Singmaster," 13; see also Kribbs, "Elsie Singmaster," 3.

4. Kribbs, "Elsie Singmaster," 35–26.

5. Singmaster, *Gettysburg,* 190.

6. Ibid., 8.

7. Ibid., 188.

8.For more on the 1913 Gettysburg commemoration and Civil War memory in general, see David Blight, *The Civil War in American Memory* (Cambridge, Mass.: Harvard University Press, 2001): 6–11, 383–97.

9. Singmaster, *Gettysburg,* 62.

10. Review of *Gettysburg* in *The Independent* 75 (July 3, 1913): 48.

11. Review of *Gettysburg* in *Review of Reviews* 48 (August 1913): 251.

12. Review of *Gettysburg* in *Booklist* 9 (June 1913): 456.

13. Review of Gettysburg in *Nation* 96 (June 26, 1913): 644.

14. Singmaster, *Gettysburg,* 186.

I
JULY THE FIRST

GETTYSBURG

I

JULY THE FIRST

FROM the kitchen to the front door, back to the kitchen, out to the little stone-fenced yard behind the house, where her children played in their quiet fashion, Mary Bowman went uneasily. She was a bright-eyed, slender person, with an intense, abounding joy in life. In her red plaid gingham dress, with its full starched skirt, she looked not much older than her ten-year-old boy.

Presently, admonishing herself sternly, she went back to her work. She sat down in a low chair by the kitchen table, and laid upon her knee a strip of thick muslin. Upon that she placed a piece of linen, which she began to scrape with a sharp knife. Gradually a soft pile of little, downy masses gathered in her lap. After a while, as though this process were

too slow, or as though she could no longer endure her bent position, she selected another
piece of linen and began to pull it to pieces,
adding the raveled threads to the pile of
lint. Suddenly, she slipped her hands under
the soft mass, and lifted it to the table. Forgetting the knife, which fell with a clatter, she
rose and went to the kitchen door.

"Children," she said, "remember you are
not to go away."

The oldest boy answered obediently.
Mounted upon a broomstick, he impersonated
General Early, who, a few days before, had
visited the town and had made requisition
upon it; and little Katy and the four-year-
old boy represented General Early's ragged
Confederates.

Their mother's bright eyes darkened as she
watched them. Those raiding Confederates
had been so terrible to look upon, so ragged,
so worn, so starving. Their eyes had been
like black holes in their brown faces; they had
had the figures of youth and the decrepitude
of age. A straggler from their ranks had told
her that the Southern men of strength and

maturity were gone, that there remained in his village in Georgia only little boys and old, old men. The Union soldiers who had come yesterday, marching in the Emmittsburg road, through the town and out to the Theological Seminary, were different; travel-worn as they were, they had seemed, in comparison, like new recruits.

Suddenly Mary Bowman clasped her hands. Thank God, they would not fight here! Once more frightened Gettysburg had anticipated a battle, once more its alarm had proved ridiculous. Early had gone days ago to York, the Union soldiers were marching toward Chambersburg. Thank God, John Bowman, her husband, was not a regular soldier, but a fifer in the brigade band. Members of the band, poor Mary thought, were safe, danger would not come nigh them. Besides, he was far away with Hooker's idle forces. No failure to give battle made Mary indignant, no reproaches of an inert general fell from her lips. She was passionately grateful that they did not fight.

It was only on dismal, rainy days, or when

she woke at night and looked at her little children lying in their beds, that the vague, strange possibility of her husband's death occurred to her. Then she assured herself with conviction that God would not let him die. They were so happy, and they were just beginning to prosper. They had paid the last upon their little house before he went to war; now they meant to save money and to educate their children. By fall the war would be over, then John would come back and resume his school-teaching, and everything would be as it had been.

She went through the kitchen again and out to the front door, and looked down the street with its scattering houses. Opposite lived good-natured, strong-armed Hannah Casey; in the next house, a dozen rods away, the Deemer family. The Deemers had had great trouble, the father was at war and the two little children were ill with typhoid fever. In a little while she would go down and help. It was still early; perhaps the children and their tired nurses slept.

Beyond, the houses were set closer together,

the Wilson house first, where a baby was watched for now each day, and next to it the McAtee house, where Grandma McAtee was dying. In that neighborhood, and a little farther on past the new court-house in the square, which Gettysburg called "The Diamond," men were moving about, some mounted, some on foot. Their presence did not disturb Mary, since Early had gone in one direction and the Union soldiers were going in the other. Probably the Union soldiers had come to town to buy food before they started on their march. She did not even think uneasily of the sick and dying; she said to herself that if the soldiers had wished to fight here, the good men of the village, the judge, the doctor, and the ministers would have gone forth to meet them and with accounts of the invalids would have persuaded them to stay away!

Over the tops of the houses, Mary could see the cupola of the Seminary lifting its graceful dome and slender pillars against the blue sky. She and her husband had always planned that one of their boys should go to the Seminary and learn to be a preacher; she remembered their hope now. Far beyond Seminary Ridge, the foothills of the Blue Ridge lay clear and purple in the morning sunshine. The sun, already high in the sky, was behind her; it stood over the tall, thick pines of the little cemetery where her kin lay, and where she herself would lie with her husband beside her. Except for that dim spot, the whole lovely landscape was unshadowed.

Suddenly she put out her hand to the pillar of the porch and called her neighbor: —

"Hannah!"

The door of the opposite house opened, and Hannah Casey's burly figure crossed the street. She had been working in her carefully tended garden and her face was crimson. Hannah Casey anticipated no battle.

"Good morning to you," she called. "What is it you want?"

"Come here," bade Mary Bowman.

The Irishwoman climbed the three steps to the little porch.

"What is it?" she asked again. "What is it you see?"

"Look! — Out there at the Seminary ! You can see the soldiers moving about, like black specks under the trees!"

Hannah squinted a pair of near-sighted eyes in the direction of the Seminary.

"I'll take your word for it," she said.

With a sudden motion Mary Bowman lifted her hand to her lips.

"Early would n't come back!" she whispered. "He would never come back!"

Hannah Casey laughed a bubbling laugh.

"Come back? Those rag-a-bones? It 'ud go hard with them if they did. The Unionists would n't jump before 'em like the rabbits here. But I did n't jump! The Bateses fled once more for their lives, it's the seventeenth time they've saved their valuable commodities from the foe. Down the street they flew, their tin dishes and their precious chiny rattling in their wagon. 'Oh, my kind sir!' says Lillian to the raggedy man you fed, — 'oh, my kind sir, I surrender!' 'You're right you do,' says he. 'We're goin' to eat you up!' — 'Lady,' says that same snip to me, 'you'd better leave your home.' 'Worm!' says I back to him, '*you* leave my home!' And you fed him, you soft-heart!''

"He ate like an animal," said Mary; "as though he had had nothing for days."

"And all the cave-dwellers was talkin' about divin' for their cellars. I was n't goin' into no cellar. Here I stay, aboveground, till they lay me out for good."

Mary Bowman laughed suddenly, hysterically. She had laughed thus far through all the sorrows war had brought, — poverty, separation, anxiety. She might still laugh; there was no danger; Early had gone in one direction, the Union soldiers in the other.

"Did you see him dive into the apple-butter, Hannah Casey? His face was smeared with it. He could n't wait till the biscuits were out of the oven. He —" She stopped and listened, frowning. She looked out once more toward the ridge with its moving spots, then down at the town with its larger spots, then back at the pines, standing straight and tall in the July sunshine. She could see the white tombstones beneath the trees.

"Listen!" she cried.

"To what?" demanded Hannah Casey.

For a few seconds the women stood silently. There were still the same faint, distant sounds, but they were not much louder, not much more numerous than could be heard in the village on any summer morning. A heart which dreaded ominous sound might have been set at rest by the peace and stillness.

Hannah Casey spoke irritably.

"What do you hear?"

"Nothing," answered Mary Bowman. "But I thought I heard men marching. I believe it's my heart beating! I thought I heard them in the night. Could you sleep?"

"Like a log!" said Hannah Casey. "Sleep? Why, of course, I could sleep! Ain't our boys yonder? Ain't the Rebs shakin' in their shoes? No, they ain't. They ain't got no shoes. Ain't the Bateses, them barometers of war, still in their castle, ain't —"

"I slept the first part of the night," interrupted Mary Bowman. "Then it seemed to me I heard men marching. I thought perhaps they were coming through the town from the hill, and I looked out, but there was nothing stirring. It was the brightest night I ever saw. I—"

Again Hannah Casey laughed her mighty laugh. There were nearer sounds now, the rattle of a cart behind them, the gallop of hoofs before. Again the Bateses were coming, a family of eight crowded into a little springless wagon with what household effects they could collect. Hannah Casey waved her apron at them and went out to the edge of the street.

"Run!" she yelled. "Skedaddle! Murder! Help! Police!"

Neither her jeers nor Mary Bowman's laugh could make the Bateses turn their heads. Mrs. Bates held in her short arms a feather bed, her children tried to get under it as chicks creep under the wings of a mother hen. Down in front of the Deemer house they stopped suddenly. A Union soldier had halted them, then let them pass. He rode his horse up on the pavement and pounded with his sword at the Deemer door.

"He might terrify the children to death!" cried Mary Bowman, starting forward.

But already the soldier was riding toward her.

"There is sickness there!" she shouted to his unheeding ears; "you ought n't to pound like that!"

"You women will have to stay in your cellars," he answered. "A battle is to be fought here."

"Here?" said Mary Bowman stupidly.

"Get out!" said Hannah Casey. "There ain't nobody here to fight with!"

The soldier rode his horse to Hannah Casey's door, and began to pound with his sword.

"I live there!" screamed Hannah. "You dare to bang that door!"

Mary Bowman crossed the street and looked up at him as he sat on his great horse.

"Oh, sir, do you mean that they will fight *here?*"

"I do."

"In Gettysburg?" Hannah Casey could scarcely speak for rage.

"In Gettysburg."

"Where there are women and children?"

screamed Hannah. "And gardens planted? I'd like to see them in my garden, I —"

"Get into your cellars," commanded the soldier. "You'll be safe there."

"Sir!" Mary Bowman went still a little closer. The crisis in the Deemer house was not yet passed, even at the best it was doubtful whether Agnes Wilson could survive the hour of her trial, and Grandma McAtee was dying. "Sir!" said Mary Bowman, earnestly, ignorant of the sublime ridiculousness of her reminder, "there are women and children here whom it might kill."

The man laughed a short laugh.

"Oh, my God!" He leaned a little from his saddle. "Listen to me, sister! I have lost my father and two brothers in this war. Get into your cellars."

With that he rode down the street.

"He's a liar," cried Hannah Casey. She started to run after him. "Go out to Peterson's field to do your fighting," she shouted furiously. "Nothing will grow there! Go out there!"

Then she stopped, panting.

The soldier took time to turn and grin and wave his hand.

"He's a liar," declared Hannah Casey once more. "Early's went. There ain't nothing to fight with."

Still scolding, she joined Mary Bowman on her porch. Mary Bowman stood looking through the house at her children, playing in the little field. They still played quietly; it seemed to her that they had never ceased to miss their father.

Then Mary Bowman looked down the street. In the Diamond the movement was more rapid, the crowd was thicker. Women had come out to the doorsteps, men were hurrying about. It seemed to Mary that she heard Mrs. Deemer scream. Suddenly there was a clatter of hoofs; a dozen soldiers, riding from the town, halted and began to question her. Their horses were covered with foam; they had come at a wild gallop from Seminary Ridge.

"This is the road to Baltimore?"

"Yes."

"Straight ahead?"

"Yes."

Gauntleted hands lifted the dusty reins.

"You'd better protect yourself! There is going to be a battle."

"Here?" asked Mary Bowman again stupidly.

"Right here."

Hannah Casey thrust herself between them.

"Who are you goin' to fight with, say?"

The soldiers grinned at her. They were already riding away.

"With the Turks," answered one over his shoulder.

Another was kinder, or more cruel.

"Sister!" he explained, "it is likely that two hundred thousand men will be engaged on this spot. The whole Army of Northern Virginia is advancing from the north, the whole Army of the Potomac is advancing from the south, you —"

The soldier did not finish. His galloping comrades had left him, he hastened to join them. After him floated another accusation of lying from the lips of Hannah Casey. Hannah was irritated because the Bateses were right.

"Hannah!" said Mary Bowman thickly. "I told you how I dreamed I heard them marching. It was as though they came in every road, Hannah, from Baltimore and Taneytown and Harrisburg and York. The roads were full of them, they were shoulder against shoulder, and their faces were like death!"

Hannah Casey grew ghastly white. Superstition did what common sense and word of man could not do.

"So you did!" she whispered; "so you did!"

Mary Bowman clasped her hands and looked about her, down the street, out toward the Seminary, back at the grim trees. The little sounds had died away; there was now a mighty stillness.

"He said the whole Army of the Potomac," she repeated. "John is in the Army of the Potomac."

"That is what he said," answered the Irishwoman.

"What will the Deemers do?" cried Mary Bowman. "And the Wilsons?"

"God knows!" said Hannah Casey.

Suddenly Mary Bowman lifted her hands above her head.

"Look!" she screamed.

"What?" cried Hannah Casey. "What is it?"

Mary Bowman went backwards toward the door, her eyes still fixed on the distant ridge, as though they could not be torn away. It was nine o'clock; a shrill little clock in the house struck the hour.

"Children!" called Mary Bowman. "Come! See!"

The children dropped the little sticks with which they played and ran to her.

"What is it?" whined Hannah Casey.

Mary Bowman lifted the little boy to her shoulder. A strange, unaccountable excitement possessed her, she hardly knew what she was doing. She wondered what a battle would be like. She did not think of wounds, or of blood or of groans, but of great sounds, of martial music, of streaming flags carried aloft. She sometimes dreamed that her husband, though he had so unimportant a place, might perform some great deed of valor, might snatch the colors from a wounded bearer, and lead his regiment to victory upon the field of battle. And now, besides, this moment, he was marching home! She never thought that he might die, that he might be lost, swallowed up in the yawning mouth of some great battle-trench; she never dreamed that she would never see him again, would hunt for him among thousands of dead bodies, would have her eyes filled with sights intolerable, with wretchedness unspeakable, would be tortured by a thousand agonies which she could not assuage, torn by a thousand griefs beside her own. She could not foresee that all the dear woods and fields which she loved, where she had played as a child, where she had picnicked as a girl, where she had walked with her lover as a young woman, would become, from Round Top to the Seminary, from the Seminary to Culp's Hill, a great shambles, then a great charnel-house. She lifted the little boy to her shoulder and held him aloft.

"See, darling!" she cried. "See the bright things sparkling on the hill!"

"What are they?" begged Hannah Casey,
trying desperately to see.

"They are bayonets and swords!"

She put the little boy down on the floor,
and looked at him.   Hannah Casey had
clutched her arm.

"Hark!" said Hannah Casey.

Far out toward the shining cupola of the
Seminary there was a sharp little sound, then
another, and another.

"What is it?" shrieked Hannah Casey.
"Oh, what is it?"

"What is it!" mocked Mary Bowman. "It
is—"

A single, thundering, echoing blast took
the words from Mary Bowman's lips.

Stupidly, she and Hannah Casey looked at
one another.

II
THE HOME-COMING

II

THE HOME-COMING

PARSONS knew little of the great wave of protest that swept over the Army of the Potomac when Hooker was replaced by Meade. The sad depression of the North, sick at heart since December, did not move him; he was too thoroughly occupied with his own sensations. He sat alone, when his comrades would leave him alone, brooding, his terror equally independent of victory or defeat. The horror of war appalled him. He tried to reconstruct the reasons for his enlisting, but found it impossible. The war had made of him a stranger to himself. He could scarcely visualize the little farm that he had left, or his mother. Instead of the farm, he saw corpse-strewn fields; instead of his mother, the mutilated bodies of young men. His senses seemed unable to respond to any other stimuli than those of war. He had not been conscious of the odors of the sweet Mary-

land spring, or of the song of mocking-birds;
his nostrils were full of the smell of blood, his
ears of the cries of dying men.

Worse than the recollection of what he had
seen were the forebodings that filled his soul.
In a day — yes, an hour, for the rumors of
coming battle forced themselves to his unwilling ears — he might be as they. Presently he
too would lie, staring, horrible, under the
Maryland sky.

The men in his company came gradually to
leave him to himself. At first they thought no
less of him because he was afraid. They had
all been afraid. They discussed their sensations frankly as they sat round the camp-fire,
or lay prone on the soft grass of the fields.

"Scared!" laughed the oldest member of
the company, who was speaking chiefly for the
encouragement of Parsons, whom he liked.
"My knees shook, and my chest caved in.
Every bullet killed me. But by the time I'd
been dead about forty times, I saw the
Johnnies, and something hot got into my
throat, and I got over it."

"And were n't you afraid afterwards?"

asked Parsons, trying to make his voice sound natural.

"No, never."

"But I was," confessed another man. His face was bandaged, and blood oozed through from the wound that would make him leer like a satyr for the rest of his life. "I get that way every time. But I get over it. I don't get hot in my throat, but my skin prickles."

Young Parsons walked slowly away, his legs shaking visibly beneath him.

Adams turned on his side and watched him.

"Got it bad," he said shortly. Then he lay once more on his back and spread out his arms. "God, but I'm sick of it! And if Lee's gone into Pennsylvania, and we're to chase him, and old Joe's put out, the Lord knows what'll become of us. I bet you a pipeful of tobacco, there ain't one of us left by this time next week. I bet you —"

The man with the bandaged face did not answer. Then Adams saw that Parsons had come back and was staring at him.

"Ain't Hooker in command no more?" he asked.

"No; Meade."

"And we're going to Pennsylvania?"

"Guess so." Adams sat upright, the expression of kindly commiseration on his face changed to one of disgust. "Brace up, boy. What's the matter with you?"

Parsons sat down beside him. His face was gray; his blue eyes, looking out from under his little forage-cap, closed as though he were swooning.

"I can't stand it," he said thickly. "I can see them all day, and hear them all night, all the groaning — I —"

The old man pulled from his pocket a little bag. It contained his last pipeful of tobacco, the one that he had been betting.

"Take that. You got to get such things out of your head. It won't do. The trouble with you is that ever since you've enlisted, this company 's been hanging round the outside. You ain't been in a battle. One battle'll cure you. You got to get over it."

"Yes," repeated the boy. "I got to get over it."

He lay down beside Adams, panting. The

"I CAN'T STAND IT," HE SAID THICKLY

moon, which would be full in a few days, had risen; the sounds of the vast army were all about them — the click of tin basin against tin basin, the stamping of horses, the oaths and laughter of men. Some even sang. The boy, when he heard them, said, "Oh, God!" It was his one exclamation. It had broken from his lips a thousand times, not as a prayer or as an imprecation, but as a mixture of both. It seemed the one word that could represent the indescribable confusion of his mind. He said again, "Oh, God! Oh, God!"

It was not until two days later, when they had been for hours on the march, that he realized that they were approaching the little Pennsylvania town where he lived. He had been marching almost blindly, his eyes nearly closed, still contemplating his own misery and fear. He could not discuss with his comrades the next day's prospects, he did not know enough about the situation to speculate. Adams's hope that there would be a battle brought to his lips the familiar "Oh, God!" He had begun to think of suicide.

It was almost dark once more when they

stumbled into a little town. Its streets, washed by rains, had been churned to thick red mud by thousands of feet and wheels. The mud clung to Parsons's worn shoes; it seemed to his half-crazy mind like blood. Then, suddenly, his gun dropped with a wild clatter to the ground.

"It's Taneytown!" he called wildly. "It's Taneytown."

Adams turned upon him irritably. He was almost too tired to move.

"What if it is Taneytown?" he thundered. " Pick up your gun, you young fool."

"But it's only ten miles from home!"

The shoulder of the man behind him sent Parsons sprawling. He gathered himself up and leaped into his place by Adams's side. His step was light.

"Ten miles from home! We're only ten miles from home!" — he said it as though the evil spirits which had beset him had been exorcised. He saw the little whitewashed farmhouse, the yellowing wheat-fields beside it; he saw his mother working in the garden, he heard her calling.

Presently he began to look furtively about him. If he could only get away, if he could get home, they could never find him. There were many places where he could hide, holes and caverns in the steep, rough slopes of Big Round Top, at whose foot stood his mother's little house. They could never find him. He began to speak to Adams tremulously.

"When do you think we'll camp?"

'Adams answered him sharply.

"Not to-night. Don't try any running-away business, boy. 'T ain't worth while. They'll shoot you. Then you'll be food for crows."

The boy moistened his parched lips.

"I did n't say anything about running away," he muttered. But hope died in his eyes.

It did not revive when, a little later, they camped in the fields, trampling the wheat ready for harvest, crushing down the corn already waist-high, devouring their rations like wolves, then falling asleep almost on their feet.

Well indeed might they sleep heavily,

dully, undisturbed by cry of picket or gallop of returning scout. The flat country lay clear and bright in the moonlight; to the northwest they could almost see the low cone of Big Round Top, to which none then gave a thought, not even Parsons himself, who lay with his tanned face turned up toward the sky. Once his sunken eyes opened, but he did not remember that now, if ever, he must steal away, over his sleeping comrades, past the picket-line, and up the long red road toward home. He thought of home no more, nor of fear; he lay like a dead man.

It was a marvelous moonlit night. All was still as though round Gettysburg lay no vast armies, seventy thousand Southerners to the north, eighty-five thousand Northerners to the south. They lay or moved quietly, like great octopi, stretching out, now and then, grim tentacles, which touched or searched vainly. They knew nothing of the quiet, academic town, lying in its peaceful valley away from the world for which it cared little. Mere chance decreed that on the morrow its name should stand beside Waterloo.

Parsons whimpered the next morning when he heard the sound of guns. He knew what would follow. In a few hours the firing would cease; then they would march, wildly seeking an enemy that seemed to have vanished, or covering the retreat of their own men; and there would be once more all the ghastly sounds and cries. But the day passed, and they were still in the red fields.

It was night when they began to march once more. All day the sounds of firing had echoed faintly from the north, bringing fierce rage to the hearts of some, fear to others, and dread unspeakable to Parsons. He did not know how the day passed. He heard the guns, he caught glimpses now and then of messengers galloping to headquarters; he sat with bent head and staring eyes. Late in the afternoon the firing ceased, and he said over and over again, "Oh, God, don't let us go that way! Oh, God, don't let us go that way!" He did not realize that the noise came from the direction of Gettysburg, he did not comprehend that "that way" meant home, he felt no anxiety for the safety of his mother; he knew only that, if he saw another dead or dying man, he himself would die. Nor would his death be simply a growing unconsciousness; he would suffer in his body all the agony of the wounds upon which he looked.

The great octopus of which he was a part did not feel in the least the spark of resistance in him, one of the smallest of the particles that made up its vast body. When the moon had risen, he was drawn in toward the centre with the great tentacle to which he belonged. The octopus suffered; other vast arms were bleeding and almost severed. It seemed to shudder with foreboding for the morrow.

Round Top grew clear before them as they marched. The night was blessedly cool and bright, and they went as though by day, but fearfully, each man's ears strained to hear. It was like marching into the crater of a volcano which, only that afternoon, had been in fierce eruption. It was all the more horrible because now they could see nothing but the clear July night, hear nothing but the soft sounds of summer. There was not even a flag of smoke to warn them.

They caught, now and again, glimpses of men hiding behind hedge-rows, then hastening swiftly away.

"Desertin'," said Adams grimly.

"What did you say?" asked Parsons.

He had heard distinctly enough, but he longed for the sound of Adams's voice. When Adams repeated the single word, Parsons did not hear. He clutched Adams by the arm.

"You see that hill, there before us?"

"Yes."

"Gettysburg is over that hill. There's the cemetery. My father's buried there."

Adams looked in under the tall pines. He could see the white stones standing stiffly in the moonlight.

"We're goin' in there," he said. "Keep your nerve up there, boy."

Adams had seen other things besides the white tombstones, things that moved faintly or lay quietly, or gave forth ghastly sounds. He was conscious, by his sense of smell, of the army about him and of the carnage that had been.

Parsons, strangely enough, had neither

heard nor smelled. A sudden awe came upon
him; the past returned: he remembered his
father, his mother's grief at his death, his
visits with her to the cemetery. It seemed to
him that he was again a boy stealing home
from a day's fishing in Rock Creek, a little
fearful as he passed the cemetery gate. He
touched Adams's arm shyly before he began
to sling off his knapsack and to lie down as
his comrades were doing all about him.

"That is my father's grave," he whispered.

Then, before the kindly answer sprang from
Adams's lips, a gurgle came into Parsons's
throat as though he were dying. One of the
apparitions that Adams had seen lifted itself
from the grass, leaving behind dark stains.
The clear moonlight left no detail of the hideous wounds to the imagination.

"Parsons!" cried Adams sharply.

But Parsons had gone, leaping over the
graves, bending low by the fences, dashing
across an open field, then losing himself in the
woodland. For a moment Adams's eyes followed him, then he saw that the cemetery
and the outlying fields were black with ten

thousand men. It would be easy for Parsons to get away.

"No hope for him," he said shortly, as he set to work to do what he could for the maimed creature at his feet. Dawn, he knew, must be almost at hand; he fancied that the moonlight was paling. He was almost crazy for sleep, sleep that he would need badly enough on the morrow, if he were any prophet of coming events.

Parsons, also, was aware of the tens of thousands of men about him, to him they were dead or dying men. He staggered as he ran, his feet following unconsciously the path that took him home from fishing, along the low ridge, past scattered farmhouses, toward the cone of Round Top. It seemed to him that dead men leaped at him and tried to stop him, and he ran ever faster. Once he shrieked, then he crouched in a fence-corner and hid. He would have been ludicrous, had the horrors from which he fled been less hideous.

He, too, felt the dawn coming, as he saw his mother's house. He sobbed like a little child, and, no longer keeping to the shade, ran across the open fields. There were no dead men here, thank God! He threw himself frantically at the door, and found it locked. Then he drew from the window the nail that held it down, and crept in. He was ravenously hungry, and his hands made havoc in the familiar cupboard. He laughed as he found cake, and the loved "drum-sticks" of his childhood.

He did not need to slip off his shoes for fear of waking his mother, for the shoes had no soles; but he stooped down and removed them with trembling hands. Then a great peace seemed to come into his soul. He crept on his hands and knees past his mother's door, and climbed to his own little room under the eaves, where, quite simply, as though he were a little boy, and not a man deserting from the army on the eve of a battle, he said his prayers and went to bed.

When he awoke, it was late afternoon. He thought at first that he had been swinging, and had fallen; then he realized that he still lay quietly in his bed. He stretched himself, reveling in the blessed softness, and wondering why he felt as though he had been brayed in a mortar. Then a roar of sound shut out possibility of thought. The little house shook with it. He covered his ears, but he might as well have spared himself his pains. That sound could never be shut out, neither then, nor for years afterward, from the ears of those who heard it. There were many who would hear no other sound forevermore. The coward began again his whining, "Oh, God! Oh, God!" His nostrils were full of smoke; he could smell already the other ghastly odors that would follow. He lifted himself from his bed, and, hiding his eyes from the window, felt his way down the steep stairway. He meant, God help him! to go and hide his face in his mother's lap. He remembered the soft, cool smoothness of her gingham apron.

Gasping, he staggered into her room. But his mother was not there. The mattress and sheets from her bed had been torn off; one sheet still trailed on the floor. He picked it up and shook it. He was imbecile enough to think she might be beneath it.

"Mother!" he shrieked. "Mother! Mother!" forgetting that even in that little room she could not have heard him. He ran through the house, shouting. Everywhere it was the same — stripped beds, cupboards flung wide, the fringe of torn curtains still hanging. His mother was not there.

His terror drove him finally to the window overlooking the garden. It was here that he most vividly remembered her, bending over her flower-beds, training the tender vines, pulling weeds. She must be here. In spite of the snarl of guns, she must be here. But the garden was a waste, the fence was down. He saw only the thick smoke beyond, out of which crept slowly toward him half a dozen men with blackened faces and blood-stained clothes, again his dead men come to life. He saw that they wore his own uniform, but the fact made little impression upon him. Was his mother dead? Had she been killed yesterday, or had they taken her away last night or this morning while he slept? He saw that the men were coming nearer to the house, creeping slowly on through the thick smoke. He wondered vaguely whether they were coming for him as they had come for his mother. Then he saw, also vaguely, on the left, another group of men, stealing toward him, men who did not wear his uniform, but who walked as bravely as his own comrades.

He knew little about tactics, and his brain was too dull to realize that the little house was the prize they sought. It was marvelous that it had remained unpossessed so long, when a tiny rock or a little bush was protection for which men struggled. The battle had surged that way; the little house was to become as famous as the Peach Orchard or the Railroad Cut, it was to be the "Parsons House" in history. Of this Parsons had no idea; he only knew, as he watched them, that his mother was gone, his house despoiled.

Then, suddenly, rage seized upon him, driving out fear. It was not rage with the men in gray, creeping so steadily upon him — he thought of them as men like himself, only a thousand times more brave — it was rage with war itself, which drove women from their homes, which turned young men into groaning apparitions. And because he felt this rage, he too must kill. He knelt down before the window, his gun in his hand. He had carried it absently with him the night before, and he had twenty rounds of ammunition. He took careful aim: his hand, thanks to his mother's food and his long sleep, was quite steady; and he pulled the trigger.

At first, both groups of men halted. The shot had gone wide. They had seen the puff of smoke, but they had no way of telling whether it was friend or foe who held the little house. There was another puff, and a man in gray fell. The men in blue hastened their steps, even yet half afraid, for the field was broad, and to cross it was madness unless the holders of the house were their own comrades. Another shot went wide, another man in gray dropped, and another, and the men in blue leaped on, yelling. Not until then did Parsons see that there were more than twice as many men in gray as men in blue. The men in gray saw also, and they, too, ran. The little house was worth tremendous risks. Another man bounded into the air and rolled over, blood spurting from his mouth, and the man behind him stumbled over him. There were only twelve now. Then there were eleven. But they came on — they were nearer than the men in blue. Then another fell, and another. It seemed to Parsons that he could go on forever watching them. He smiled grimly at the queer antics that they cut, the strange postures into which they threw themselves. Then another fell, and they wavered and turned. One of the men in blue stopped at the edge of the garden to take deliberate aim, but Parsons, grinning, also leveled his gun once more. He wondered, a little jealously, which of them had killed the man in gray.

The six men, rushing in, would not believe that he was there alone. They looked at him, admiringly, grim, bronzed as they were, the veterans of a dozen battles. They did not think of him for an instant as a boy; his eyes were the eyes of a man who had suffered and who had known the hot pleasures of revenge. It was he who directed them now in fortifying the house, he who saw the first sign of the creeping Confederates making another sally from the left, he who led them into the

woods when, reinforced by a hundred of their
comrades, they used the little house only as a
base toward which to retreat. They had never
seen such fierce rage as his. The sun sank behind the Blue Ridge, and he seemed to regret
that the day of blood was over. He was not
satisfied that they held the little house; he
must venture once more into the dark shad-
ows of the woodland.

From there his new-found comrades dragged
him helpless. His enemies, powerless against
him by day, had waited until he could not see
them. His comrades carried him into the
house, where they had made a dim light.
The smoke of battle seemed to be lifting;
there was still sharp firing, but it was silence
compared to what had been, peace compared
to what would be on the morrow.

They laid him on the floor of the little
kitchen, and looked at the wide rent in his
neck, and lifted his limp arm, not seeing that
a door behind them had opened quietly,
and that a woman had come up from the deep
cellar beneath the house. There was not a
cellar within miles that did not shelter fright-

ened women and children. Parsons's mother, warned to flee, had gone no farther. She appeared now, a ministering angel. In her cellar was food in plenty; there were blankets, bandages, even pillows for bruised and aching heads. Heaven grant that some one would thus care for her boy in the hour of his need!

The men watched Parsons's starting eyes, thinking they saw death. They would not have believed that it was Fear that had returned upon him, their brave captain. They would have said that he never could have been afraid. He put his hand up to his torn throat. His breath came in thick gasps. He muttered again, "Oh, God! Oh, God!"

Then, suddenly, incomprehensibly to the men who did not see the gracious figure behind them, peace ineffable came into his blue eyes.

"Why, *mother!*" he said softly.

III
VICTORY

III

VICTORY [1]

SITTING his horse easily in the stone-
fenced field near the rounded clump of
trees on the hot noon of the third day of battle,
his heart leaping, sure of the righteousness of
his cause, sure of the overruling providence
of God, experienced in war, trained to obed-
dience, accustomed to command, the young
officer looked about him.

To his right and left and behind him, from
Culp's Hill to Round Top, lay the Army of
the Potomac, the most splendid army, in his
opinion, which the world had ever seen, an
army tried, proved, reliable in all things. The
first day's defeat, the second day's victory,

[1] From the narrative of Colonel Frank Aretas Haskell,
Thirty-sixth Wisconsin Infantry. While aide-de-camp to
General Gibbon he was largely instrumental in saving the
day at Gettysburg to the Union forces. His brilliant story
of the battle is contained in a series of letters written to his
brother soon after the contest.

were past; since yesterday the battle-lines had been re-formed; upon them the young man looked with approval, thanking Heaven for Meade. The lines were arranged, except here in the very centre near this rounded clump of trees where he waited, as he would have arranged them himself, conformably to the ground, batteries in place, infantry — there a double, here a single line — to the front. There had been ample time for such re-formation during the long, silent morning. Now each man was in his appointed place, munition-wagons and ambulances waited, regimental flags streamed proudly; everywhere was order, composure. The laughter and joking which floated to the ears of the young officer betokened also minds composed, at ease. Yesterday twelve thousand men had been killed or wounded upon this field; the day before yesterday, eleven thousand; to-day, this afternoon, within a few hours, eight thousand more would fall. Yet, lightly, their arms stacked, men laughed, and the young officer heard them with approval.

Opposite, on another ridge, a mile away,

Lee's army waited. They, too, were set out in brave array; they, too, had re-formed; they, too, seemed to have forgotten yesterday, to have closed their eyes to to-morrow. From the rounded clump of trees, the young officer could look across the open fields, straight to the enemy's centre. Again he wished for a double line of troops here about him. But Meade alone had power to place them there.

The young officer was cultivated, college-bred, with the gift of keen observation, of vivid expression. The topography of that varied country was already clear to him; he was able to draw a sketch of it, indicating its steep hills, its broad fields, its tracts of virgin woodland, the "wave-like" crest upon which he now stood. He could not have written so easily during the marches of the succeeding weeks if he had not now, in the midst of action, begun to fit words to what he saw. He watched Meade ride down the lines, his face "calm, serious, earnest, without arrogance of hope or timidity of fear." He shared with his superiors in a hastily prepared,

delicious lunch, eaten on the ground; he recorded it with humorous impressions of these
great soldiers.

The evening before he had attended them
in their council of war; he has made it as plain
to us as though we, too, had been inside that
little farmhouse. It is a picture in which Rem-
brandt would have delighted, — the low room,
the little table with its wooden water-pail,
its tin cup, its dripping candle. We can see
the yellow light on blue sleeves, on soft,
slouched, gilt-banded hats, on Gibbon's single
star. Meade, tall, spare, sinewy; Sedgwick,
florid, thick-set; young Howard with his
empty sleeve; magnificent Hancock, — of all
that distinguished company the young officer
has drawn imperishable portraits.

He heard their plans, heard them decide to
wait until the enemy had hurled himself
upon them; he said with satisfaction that
their heads were sound. He recorded also
that when the council was over and the chance
for sleep had come, he could hardly sit his
horse for weariness, as he sought his general's
headquarters in the sultry, starless midnight.

Yet, now, in the hot noon of the third day, as he dismounted and threw himself down in the shade, he remembered the sound of the moving ambulances, the twinkle of their unsteady lamps.

Lying prone, his hat tilted over his eyes, he smiled drowsily. It was impossible to tell at what moment battle would begin, but now there was infinite peace everywhere. The young men of his day loved the sounding poetry of Byron; it is probable that he thought of the "mustering squadron," of the "marshaling in arms," of "battle's magnificently-stern array." Trained in the classics he must have remembered lines from other glorious histories. "Stranger," so said Leonidas, "stranger, go tell it in Lacedæmon that we died here in defense of her laws." "The glory of Miltiades will not let me sleep!" cried the youth of Athens. A line of Virgil the young officer wrote down afterwards in his account, thinking of weary marches: "Forsan et hæc olim meminisse juvabit." — "Perchance even these things it will be delightful hereafter to remember."

Thus while he lay there, the noon droned on. Having hidden their wounds, ignoring their losses, having planted their guidons and loaded their guns, the thousands waited.

Still dozing, the young officer looked at his watch. Once more he thought of the centre and wished that it were stronger; then he stretched out his arms to sleep. It was five minutes of one o'clock. Near him his general rested also, and with them both time moved heavily.

Drowsily he closed his eyes, comfortably he lay. Then, suddenly, at a distinct, sharp sound from the enemy's line he was awake, on his feet, staring toward the west. Before his thoughts were collected, he could see the smoke of the bursting shell; before he and his fellow officers could spring to their saddles, before they could give orders, the iron rain began about the low, wave-like crest. The breast of the general's orderly was torn open, he plunged face downward, the horses which he held galloped away. Not an instant passed after that first shot before the Union guns answered, and battle had begun.

It opened without fury, except the fury of sound, it proceeded with dignity, with majesty. There was no charge; that fierce, final on-rush was yet hours away; the little stone wall near that rounded clump of trees, over which thousands would fight, close-pressed like wrestlers, was to be for a long time unstained by blood. The Confederate aggressor, standing in his place, delivered his hoarse challenge; his Union antagonist standing also in his place, returned thunderous answer. The two opposed each other — if one may use for passion so terrible this light comparison — at arm's length, like fencers in a play.

The business of the young officer was not with these cannon, but with the infantry, who, crouching before the guns, hugging the ground, were to bide their time in safety for two hours. Therefore, sitting on his horse, he still fitted words to his thoughts. The conflict before him is not a fight for men, it is a fight for mighty engines of war; it is not a human battle, it is a storm, far above earthly passion. "Infuriate demons" are these guns, their mouths are ablaze with smoky tongues

of livid fire, their breath is murky, sulphur-
laden; they are surrounded by grimy, shouting, frenzied creatures who are not their
masters but their ministers. Around them
rolls the smoke of Hades. To their sound all
other cannonading of the young officer's experience was as a holiday salute. Solid shot
shattered iron of gun and living trunk of tree.
Shot struck also its intended target: men fell,
torn, mangled; horses started, stiffened, crashed
to the ground, or rushed, maddened, away.

Still there was nothing for the young officer
to do but to watch. Near him a man crouched
by a stone, like a toad, or like pagan wor-
shiper before his idol. The young officer
looked at him curiously.

"Go to your regiment and be a man!" he
ordered.

But the man did not stir, the shot which
splintered the protecting stone left him still
kneeling, still unhurt. To the young officer he
was one of the unaccountable phenomena of
battle, he was incomprehensible, monstrous.

He noted also the curious freaks played by
round shot, the visible flight of projectiles

through the air, their strange hiss "with
sound of hot iron, plunged into water." He
saw ambulances wrecked as they moved along;
he saw frantic horses brought down by shells;
he calls them "horse-tamers of the upper
air." He saw shells fall into limber-boxes, he
heard the terrific roar which followed louder
than the roar of guns; he observed the fall of
officer, of orderly, of private soldier.

After the first hour of terrific din, he rode
with his general down the line. The infantry
still lay prone upon the ground, out of range
of the missiles. The men were not suffering
and they were quiet and cool. They professed
not to mind the confusion; they claimed
laughingly to like it.

From the shelter of a group of trees the
young officer and his general watched in silence. For that "awful universe of battle,"
it seemed now that all other expressions were
feeble, mean. The general expostulated with
frightened soldiers who were trying to hide
near by. He did not reprove or command,
he reminded them that they were in the hands
of God, and therefore as safe in one place as

another. He assured his young companion of his own faith in God.

Slowly, after an hour and a half, the roar of battle abated, and the young officer and his general made their way back along the line. By three o'clock the great duel was over; the two hundred and fifty guns, having been fired rapidly for two hours, seemed to have become mortal, and to suffer a mortal's exhaustion. Along the crest, battery-men leaned upon their guns, gasped, and wiped the grime and sweat from their faces.

Again there was deep, ominous silence. Of the harm done on the opposite ridge they could know nothing with certainty. They looked about, then back at each other questioningly. Here disabled guns were being taken away, fresh guns were being brought up. The Union lines had suffered harm, but not irreparable harm. That centre for which the young officer had trembled was still safe. Was the struggle over? Would the enemy withdraw? Had yesterday's defeat worn him out; was this great confusion intended to cover his retreat? Was it —

Suddenly, madly, the young officer and his general flung themselves back into their saddles, wildly they galloped to the summit of that wave-like crest.

What they saw there was incredible, yet real; it was impossible, yet it was visible. How far had the enemy gone in the retreat which they suspected? The enemy was at hand. What of their speculations about his withdrawal, of their cool consideration of his intention? In five minutes he would be upon them. From the heavy smoke he issued, regiment after regiment, brigade after brigade, his front half a mile broad, his ranks shoulder to shoulder, line supporting line. His eyes were fixed upon that rounded clump of trees, his course was directed toward the centre of that wave-like crest. He was eighteen thousand against six thousand; should his gray mass enter, wedge-like, the Union line, yesterday's Union victories, day before yesterday's Union losses would be in vain.

To the young officer, enemies though they were, they seemed admirable. They had but one soul; they would have been, under a less deadly fire, opposed by less fearful odds, an irresistible mass. Before them he saw their galloping officers, their scarlet flags; he discerned their gun-barrels and bayonets gleaming in the sun.

His own army was composed also; it required no orders, needed no command; it knew well what that gray wall portended. He heard the click of gun-locks, the clang of muskets, raised to position upon the stone wall, the clink of iron axles, the words of his general, quiet, calm, cool.

"Do not hurry! Let them come close! Aim low and steadily!"

There came to him a moment of fierce rapture. He saw the color-sergeant tipping his lance toward the enemy; he remembered that from that glorious flag, lifted by the western breeze, these advancing hosts would filch half its stars. With bursting heart, blessing God who had kept him loyal, he determined that this thing should not be.

He was sent to Meade to announce the coming of the foe; he returned, galloping along the crest. Into that advancing army the

Union cannon poured shells; then, as the range grew shorter, shrapnel; then, canister; and still the hardy lines moved on. There was no charging shout, there was still no confusion, no halt under that raking fire. Stepping over the bodies of their friends, they continued to advance, they raised their muskets, they fired. There was now a new sound, "like summer hail upon the city roofs."

The young officer searched for his general, and could not find him. He had been mounted; now, probably wounded, possibly killed, he was down from his horse.

Then, suddenly, once more, the impossible, the incredible became possible, real. The young officer had not dreamed that the Confederates would be able to advance to the Union lines; his speculation concerned only the time they would be able to stand the Union fire. But they have advanced, they are advancing still farther. And there in that weak centre — he cannot trust his own vision — men are leaving the sheltering wall; without order or reason, a "fear-stricken flock of confusion," they are falling back. The fate of

Gettysburg, it seemed to his horrified eyes,
hung by a spider's single thread.

"A great, magnificent passion" — thus in
his youthful emotion he describes it — came
upon the young man. Danger had seemed to
him throughout a word without meaning.
Now, drawing his sword, laying about with
it, waving it in the air, shouting, he rushed
upon this fear-stricken flock, commanded it,
reproached it, cheered it, urged it back. Already the red flags had begun to thicken and
to flaunt over the deserted spot; they were
to him, he wrote afterwards, like red to a
maddened bull. That portion of the wall was
lost; he groaned for the presence of Gibbon,
of Hays, of Hancock, of Doubleday, but they
were engaged, or they were too far away. He
rushed hither and yon, still beseeching, com-
manding, praying that troops be sent to that
imperiled spot.

Then, in joy which was almost insanity,
he saw that gray line begin to waver and to
break. Tauntingly he shouted, fiercely his
men roared; than their mad yells no Confederate "Hi-yi" was ever more ferocious. This

repelling host was a new army, sprung Phœnix-like from the body of the old; to him its eyes seemed to stream lightning, it seemed to shake its wings over the yet glowing ashes of its progenitor. He watched the jostling, swaying lines, he saw them boil and roar, saw them dash their flamy spray above the crest like two hostile billows of a fiery ocean.

Once more commands are few, men do not heed them. Clearly once more they see their duty, magnificently they obey. This is war at the height of its passion, war at the summit of its glory. A color-sergeant rushed to the stone wall, there he fell; eagerly at once his comrades plunged forward. There was an instant of fierce conflict, of maddening, indistinguishable confusion. Men wrestled with one another, opposed one another with muskets used as clubs, tore at each other like wolves, until spent, exhausted, among heaps of dead, the conquered began to give themselves up. Back and forth over twenty-five square miles they had fought, for three interminable days. Here on this little crest, by this little wall, the fight was ended. Here the high-water mark was reached, here the flood began its ebb. Laughing, shouting, "so that the deaf could have seen it in their faces, the blind have heard it in their voices," the conquerors proclaimed the victory. Thank God, the crest is safe!

Are men wounded and broken by the thousands, do they lie in burning thirst, pleading for water, pleading for the bandaging of bleeding arteries, pleading for merciful death? The conquerors think of none of these things. Is night coming, are long marches coming? Still the conquerors shout like mad. Is war ended by this mammoth victory? For months and months it will drag on. Is this conquered foe a stranger, will he now withdraw to a distant country? He is our brother, his ills are ours, these wounds which we have given, we shall feel ourselves for fifty years. Is this brave young officer to enjoy the reward of his great courage, to live in fame, to be honored by his countrymen? At Cold Harbor he is to perish with a bullet in his forehead. Is not all this business of war mad?

It is a feeble, peace-loving, fireside-living generation which asks such questions as these.

Now, thank God, *the crest is safe!*

IV
THE BATTLE-GROUND

IV

THE BATTLE-GROUND

MERCIFULLY, Mary Bowman, a widow, whose husband had been missing since the battle of Gettysburg, had been warned, together with the other citizens of Gettysburg, that on Thursday the nineteenth of November, 1863, she would be awakened from sleep by a bugler's reveillé, and that during that great day she would hear again the dread sound of cannon.

Nevertheless, hearing again the reveillé, she sat up in bed with a scream and put her hands over her ears. Then, gasping, groping about in her confusion and terror, she rose and began to dress. She put on a dress which had been once a bright plaid, but which now, having lost both its color and the stiff, outstanding quality of the skirts of '63, hung about her in straight and dingy folds. It was clean, but it had upon it certain ineradicable brown stains on which soap and water seemed to have had no effect. She was thin and pale, and her eyes had a set look, as though they saw other sights than those directly about her.

In the bed from which she had risen lay her little daughter; in a trundle-bed near by, her two sons, one about ten years old, the other about four. They slept heavily, lying deep in their beds, as though they would never move. Their mother looked at them with her strange, absent gaze; then she barred a little more closely the broken shutters, and went down the stairs. The shutters were broken in a curious fashion. Here and there they were pierced by round holes, and one hung from a single hinge. The window-frames were without glass, the floor was without carpet, the beds without pillows.

In her kitchen Mary Bowman looked about her as though still seeing other sights. Here, too, the floor was carpetless. Above the stove a patch of fresh plaster on the wall showed where a great rent had been filled in; in the doors were the same little round holes as in the shutters of the room above. But there was food and fuel, which was more than one might have expected from the aspect of the house and its mistress. She opened the shattered door of the cupboard, and, having made the fire, began to prepare breakfast.

Outside the house there was already, at six o'clock, noise and confusion. Last evening a train from Washington had brought to the village Abraham Lincoln; for several days other trains had been bringing less distinguished guests, until thousands thronged the little town. This morning the tract of land between Mary Bowman's house and the village cemetery was to be dedicated for the burial of the Union dead, who were to be laid there in sweeping semicircles round a centre on which a great monument was to rise.

But of the dedication, of the President of the United States, of his distinguished associates, of the great crowds, of the soldiers, of the crape-banded banners, Mary Bowman and her children would see nothing. Mary Bowman would sit in her little wrecked kitchen with her children. For to her the President

of the United States and others in high places
who prosecuted war or who tolerated war,
who called for young men to fight, were hate-
ful. To Mary Bowman the crowds of curious
persons who coveted a sight of the great
battle-fields were ghouls; their eyes wished to
gloat upon ruin, upon fragments of the weap-
ons of war, upon torn bits of the habiliments
of soldiers; their feet longed to sink into the
loose ground of hastily made graves; the discovery of a partially covered body was precious to them.

Mary Bowman knew that field! From
Culp's Hill to the McPherson farm, from Big
Round Top to the poorhouse, she had traveled
it, searching, searching, with frantic, insane
disregard of positions or of possibility. Her
husband could not have fallen here among
the Eleventh Corps, he could not lie here
among the unburied dead of the Louisiana
Tigers! If he was in the battle at all, it was at
the Angle that he fell.

She had not been able to begin her search
immediately after the battle because there
were forty wounded men in her little house;

she could not prosecute it with any diligence even later, when the soldiers had been carried to the hospitals, in the Presbyterian Church, the Catholic Church, the two Lutheran churches, the Seminary, the College, the Court-House, and the great tented hospital on the York road. Nurses were here, Sisters of Mercy were here, compassionate women were here by the score; but still she was needed, with all the other women of the village, to nurse, to bandage, to comfort, to pray with those who must die. Little Mary Bowman had assisted at the amputation of limbs, she had helped to control strong men torn by the frenzy of delirium, she had tended poor bodies which had almost lost all semblance to humanity. Neither she nor any of the other women of the village counted themselves especially heroic; the delicate wife of the judge, the petted daughter of the doctor, the gently bred wife of the preacher forgot that fainting at the sight of blood was one of the distinguishing qualities of their sex; they turned back their sleeves and repressed their tears, and, shoulder to shoulder with Mary Bowman and her Irish neighbor, Hannah Casey, they fed the hungry and healed the sick and clothed the naked. If Mary Bowman had been herself, she might have laughed at the sight of her dresses cobbled into trousers, her skirts wrapped round the shoulders of sick men. But neither then nor ever after did Mary laugh at any incident of that summer.

Hannah Casey laughed, and by and by she began to boast. Meade, Hancock, Slocum, were non-combatants beside her. She had fought whole companies of Confederates, she had wielded bayonets, she had assisted at the spiking of a gun, she was Barbara Frietchie and Moll Pitcher combined. But all her lunacy could not make Mary Bowman smile.

Of John Bowman no trace could be found. No one could tell her anything about him, to her frantic letters no one responded. Her old friend, the village judge, wrote letters also, but could get no reply. Her husband was missing; it was probable that he lay somewhere upon this field, the field upon which they had wandered as lovers.

In midsummer a few trenches were opened,

and Mary, unknown to her friends, saw them opened. At the uncovering of the first great pit, she actually helped with her own hands. For those of this generation who know nothing of war, that fact may be written down, to be passed over lightly. The soldiers, having been on other battle-fields, accepted her presence without comment. She did not cry, she only helped doggedly, and looked at what they found. That, too, may be written down for a generation which has not known war.

Immediately, an order went forth that no graves, large or small, were to be opened before cold weather. The citizens were panic-stricken with fear of an epidemic; already there were many cases of dysentery and typhoid. Now that the necessity for daily work for the wounded was past, the village became nervous, excited, irritable. Several men and boys were killed while trying to open unexploded shells; their deaths added to the general horror. There were constant visitors who sought husbands, brothers, sweethearts; with these the Gettysburg women were still able to weep, for them they were

still able to care; but the constant demand
for entertainment for the curious annoyed
those who wished to be left alone to recover
from the shock of battle. Gettysburg was
prostrate, bereft of many of its wordly pos-
sessions, drained to the bottom of its well of
sympathy. Its schools must be opened, its
poor must be helped. Cold weather was coming and there were many, like Mary Bowman,
who owned no longer any quilts or blankets,
who had given away their clothes, their linen,
even the precious sheets which their grand-
mothers had spun. Gettysburg grudged nothing, wished nothing back, it asked only to
be left in peace.

When the order was given to postpone the
opening of graves till fall, Mary began to go
about the battle-field searching alone. Her
good, obedient children stayed at home in the
house or in the little field. They were beginning to grow thin and wan, they were shivering
in the hot August weather, but their mother
did not see. She gave them a great deal more
to eat than she had herself, and they had far
better clothes than her blood-stained motley.

She went about the battle-field with her
eyes on the ground, her feet treading gently,
anticipating loose soil or some sudden ob-
stacle. Sometimes she stooped suddenly. To
fragments of shells, to bits of blue or gray
cloth, to cartridge belts or broken muskets, she
paid no heed; at sight of pitiful bits of human
bodies she shuddered. But there lay also upon
that field little pocket Testaments, letters,
trinkets, photographs. John had had her pho-
tograph and the children's, and surely he must
have had some of the letters she had written!

But poor Mary found nothing.

One morning, late in August, she sat beside
her kitchen table with her head on her arm.
The first of the scarlet gum leaves had begun
to drift down from the shattered trees; it
would not be long before the ground would
be covered, and those depressed spots, those
tiny wooden headstones, those fragments
of blue and gray be hidden. The thought
smothered her. She did not cry, she had not
cried at all. Her soul seemed hardened, stiff,
like the terrible wounds for which she had
helped to care.

Suddenly, hearing a sound, Mary had looked up. The judge stood in the doorway; he had known all about her since she was a little girl; something in his face told her that he knew also of her terrible search. She did not ask him to sit down, she said nothing at all. She had been a loquacious person, she had become an abnormally silent one. Speech hurt her.

The judge looked round the little kitchen. The rent in the wall was still unmended, the chairs were broken; there was nothing else to be seen but the table and the rusty stove and the thin, friendless-looking children standing by the door. It was the house not only of poverty and woe, but of neglect.

"Mary," said the judge, "how do you mean to live?"

Mary's thin, sunburned hand stirred a little as it lay on the table.

"I do not know."

"You have these children to feed and clothe and you must furnish your house again. Mary —" The judge hesitated for a moment. John Bowman had been a school-teacher, a

thrifty, ambitious soul, who would have
thought it a disgrace for his wife to earn her
living. The judge laid his hand on the thin
hand beside him. "Your children must have
food, Mary. Come down to my house, and
my wife will give you work. Come now."

Slowly Mary had risen from her chair, and
smoothed down her dress and obeyed him.
Down the street they went together, seeing
fences still prone, seeing walls torn by shells,
past the houses where the shock of battle had
hastened the deaths of old persons and little
children, and had disappointed the hearts of
those who longed for a child, to the judge's
house in the square. There wagons stood
about, loaded with wheels of cannon, fragments of burst caissons, or with long, narrow,
pine boxes, brought from the railroad, to be
stored against the day of exhumation. Men
were laughing and shouting to one another,
the driver of the wagon on which the long
boxes were piled cracked his whip as he
urged his horses.

Hannah Casey congratulated her neighbor
heartily upon her finding work.

"That'll fix you up," she assured her.

She visited Mary constantly, she reported to her the news of the war, she talked at length of the coming of the President.

"I'm going to see him," she announced. "I'm going to shake him by the hand. I'm going to say, 'Hello, Abe, you old rail-splitter, God bless you!' Then the bands'll play, and the people will march, and the Johnny Rebs will hear 'em in their graves."

Mary Bowman put her hands over her ears.

"I believe in my soul you'd let 'em all rise from the dead!"

"I would!" said Mary Bowman hoarsely. "I would!"

"Well, not so Hannah Casey! Look at me garden tore to bits! Look at me beds, stripped to the ropes!"

And Hannah Casey departed to her house.

Details of the coming celebration penetrated to the ears of Mary Bowman whether she wished it or not, and the gathering crowds made themselves known. They stood upon her porch, they examined the broken shutters, they wished to question her. But Mary Bowman would answer no questions, would not let herself be seen. To her the thing was horrible. She saw the battling hosts, she heard once more the roar of artillery, she smelled the smoke of battle, she was torn by its confusion. Besides, she seemed to feel in the ground beneath her a feebly stirring, suffering, ghastly host. They had begun again to open the trenches, and she had looked into them.

Now, on the morning of Thursday, the nineteenth of November, her children dressed themselves and came down the steps. They had begun to have a little plumpness and color, but the dreadful light in their mother's eyes was still reflected in theirs. On the lower step they hesitated, looking at the door. Outside stood the judge, who had found time in the multiplicity of his cares, to come to the little house.

He spoke with kind but firm command.

"Mary," said he, "you must take these children to hear President Lincoln."

"What!" cried Mary.

"You must take these children to the exercises."

"I cannot!" cried Mary. "I cannot! I cannot!"

"You must!" The judge came into the room. "Let me hear no more of this going about. You are a Christian, your husband was a Christian. Do you want your children to think it is a wicked thing to die for their country? Do as I tell you, Mary."

Mary got up from her chair, and put on her children all the clothes they had, and wrapped about her own shoulders a little black coat which the judge's wife had given her. Then, as one who steps into an unfriendly sea, she started out with them into the great crowd. Once more, poor Mary said to herself, she would obey. She had seen the platform; by going round through the citizen's cemetery she could get close to it.

The November day was bright and warm, but Mary and her children shivered. Slowly she made her way close to the platform, patiently she stood and waited. Sometimes she stood with shut eyes, swaying a little. On the moonlit night of the third day of battle she had ventured from her house down toward the square to try to find some brandy for the dying men about her, and as in a dream she had seen a tall general, mounted upon a white horse with muffled hoofs, ride down the street. Bending from his saddle he had spoken, apparently to the empty air.

"Up, boys, up!"

There had risen at his command thousands of men lying asleep on pavement and street, and quietly, in an interminable line, they had stolen out like dead men toward the Seminary, to join their comrades and begin the long, long march to Hagerstown. It seemed to her that all about her dead men might rise now to look with reproach upon these strangers who disturbed their rest.

The procession was late, the orator of the day was delayed, but still Mary waited, swaying a little in her place. Presently the great guns roared forth a welcome, the bands played, the procession approached. On horseback, erect, gauntleted, the President of the United States drew rein beside the platform, and, with the orator and the other famous men, dismounted. There were great cheers,

there were deep silences, there were fresh
volleys of artillery, there was new music.

Of it all, Mary Bowman heard but little.
Remembering the judge, whom she saw now
near the President, she tried to obey the spirit
as well as the letter of his command; she directed her children to look, she turned their
heads toward the platform.

Men spoke and prayed and sang, and
Mary stood still in her place. The orator of
the day described the battle, he eulogized the
dead, he proved the righteousness of this
great war; his words fell upon Mary's ears
unheard. If she had been asked who he was,
she might have said vaguely that he was Mr.
Lincoln. When he ended, she was ready to
go home. There was singing; now she could
slip away, through the gaps in the cemetery
fence. She had done as the judge commanded
and now she would go back to her house.

With her arms about her children, she
started away. Then some one who stood
near by took her by the hand.

"Madam!" said he, "the President is going to speak!"

Half turning, Mary looked back. The thunder of applause made her shiver, made her even scream, it was so like that other thunderous sound which she would hear forever. She leaned upon her little children heavily, trying to get her breath, gasping, trying to keep her consciousness. She fixed her eyes upon the rising figure before her, she clung to the sight of him as a drowning swimmer in deep waters, she struggled to fix her thoughts upon him. Exhaustion, grief, misery threatened to engulf her, she hung upon him in desperation.

Slowly, as one who is old or tired or sick at heart, he rose to his feet, the President of the United States, the Commander-in-Chief of the Army and Navy, the hope of his country. Then he stood waiting. In great waves of sound the applause rose and died and rose again. He waited quietly. The winner of debate, the great champion of a great cause, the veteran in argument, the master of men, he looked down upon the throng. The clear, simple things he had to say were ready in his mind, he had thought them out, written out a first draft of them in Washington, copied it here in Gettysburg. It is probable that now, as he waited to speak, his mind traveled to other things, to the misery, the wretchedness, the slaughter of this field, to the tears of mothers, the grief of widows, the orphaning of little children.

Slowly, in his clear voice, he said what little he had to say. To the weary crowd, settling itself into position once more, the speech seemed short; to the cultivated who had been listening to the elaborate periods of great oratory, it seemed commonplace, it seemed a speech which any one might have made. But it was not so with Mary Bowman, nor with many other unlearned persons. Mary Bowman's soul seemed to smooth itself out like a scroll, her hands lightened their clutch on her children, the beating of her heart slackened, she gasped no more.

She could not have told exactly what he said, though later she read it and learned it and taught it to her children and her children's children. She only saw him, felt him, breathed him in, this great, common, kindly man. His gaze seemed to rest upon her; it was not impossible, it was even probable, that during the hours that had passed he had singled out that little group so near him, that desolate woman in her motley dress, with her children clinging about her. He said that the world would not forget this field, these martyrs; he said it in words which Mary Bowman could understand, he pointed to a future for which there was a new task.

"Daughter!" he seemed to say to her from the depths of trouble, of responsibility, of care greater than her own, — "Daughter, be of good comfort!"

Unhindered now, amid the cheers, across ground which seemed no longer to stir beneath her feet, Mary Bowman went back to her house. There, opening the shutters, she bent and solemnly kissed her little children, saying to herself that henceforth they must have more than food and raiment; they must be given some joy in life.

V

GUNNER CRISWELL

V

GUNNER CRISWELL

O N an afternoon in late September, 1910, a shifting crowd, sometimes numbering a few score, sometimes a few hundred, stared at a massive monument on the battle-field of Gettysburg. The monument was not yet finished, sundry statues were lacking, and the ground about it was trampled and bare. But the main edifice was complete, the plates, on which were cast the names of all the soldiers from Pennsylvania who had fought in the battle, were in place, and near at hand the platform, erected for the dedicatory services on the morrow, was being draped with flags. The field of Gettysburg lacks no tribute which can be paid its martyrs.

The shifting crowd was part of the great army of veterans and their friends who had begun to gather for the dedication; these had come early to seek out their names, fixed firmly in enduring bronze on the great monument. Among them were two old men. The name of one was Criswell; he had been a gunner in Battery B, and was now blind. The explosion which had paralyzed the optic nerve had not disfigured him; his smooth-shaven face in its frame of thick, white hair was unmarred, and with his erect carriage and his strong frame he was extraordinarily handsome. The name of his friend, bearded, untidy, loquacious, was Carolus Depew.

Gettysburg opens wide not only its hospitable arms, but its heart, to the old soldier. Even now, after almost fifty years, the shadow of war is not yet fled away, the roaring of the guns of battle is not stilled. The old soldier finds himself appreciated, admired, cared for, beyond a merely adequate return for the money he brings into the town. Here he can talk of the battle with the proprietor of the hotel at which he stays, with the college professor, with the urchin on the street. Any citizen will leave his work to help find a certain house where wounds were dressed, or where women gave out bread, fresh and hot from the oven; or a certain well, from which life-saving, delicious drinks were quaffed. When there are great excursions or dedications such as this, the town is decorated, there is waving of flags, there are bursts of song.

No stretching of hospitable arms could shelter the vast crowd which gathered upon this occasion. The boarding-houses which accommodated ten guests during the ordinary summer traffic now took thirty, the hotels set up as many cot-beds as their halls would hold, the students of the college and the theological seminary shared their rooms or gave them up entirely, in faculty houses every room was filled, and all church doors were thrown wide. Yet many men — and old men — spent the night upon the street.

Gunner Criswell wondered often whether many lives ran like his, up and up to a sharp peak of happiness, then plunged down, down to inexpressible misery. As a boy he had been intensely happy, eager, ambitious, alive to all the glory of the world. He had married the girl whom he loved, and had afterward enlisted, scorning any fears that he might not return. On the second day of July, 1863, on his twenty-third birthday, he had lost his sight in an explosion on the battle-field of Gettysburg; on the same day his young wife had died in their faraway corner of the state, leaving a helpless baby to a blind and sick father.

To-day the daughter was middle-aged, the father old. They lived together on their little farm in Greene County, Ellen managing the farm and doing much of the work, Gunner Criswell making baskets. War had taken his sight, his wife, all his prospects for life; it had left him, he said, Ellen, and the fresh, clear mountain air, a strong pair of hands, and his own soul. Life had settled at last to a quiet level of peace. He had learned to read the raised language of the blind, but he could not afford many books. He was poor; owing to an irregularity in his enlistment the Government had not given him a pension, nor had any one taken the trouble to have the matter straightened out. The community was small and scattered, few persons knew him, and no Congressman needed his vote in that solidly Republican district. Nor was he entirely certain that the giving of pensions to those who

could work was not a form of pauperization.
He, for instance, had been pretty well handi-
capped, yet he had got on. He said to himself
often that when one went to war one offered
everything. If there was in his heart any faint,
lingering bitterness because his country had
done nothing for him, who had given her so
much, he checked it sternly.

And, besides, he said often to himself with
amusement, he had Carolus Depew!

It was Carolus who had told him, one evening in July, about the Pennsylvania monument. Carolus had served in a different regiment, without injury and with a thousand
brave adventures. He was talking about them
now.

"I'm going! I'm going back to that place.
I could find it. I know where I knocked that
feller down with the butt of my gun when my
ammunition gave out. I know exactly where
I stood when the captain said, 'Give 'em
hell, Carolus!' The captain and me, we was
pretty intimate."

The blind man smiled, his busy hands going
on with their unending work. When he

smiled, his face was indescribably beautiful; one's heart ached for the woman who fifty years ago had had to die and leave him.

"Ellen!" he called.

Ellen appeared in the doorway, in her short, unbecoming gingham dress. She had inherited none of her father's beauty, and the freshness of her youth was gone. She looked at her father kindly enough, but her voice was harsh. Ellen's life, too, had suffered from war.

"Ellen, Carolus wants me to go with him to Gettysburg in September. A great monument is to be dedicated, and Carolus says our names are to be on it. May I go?"

Ellen turned swiftly away. Sometimes her father's cheerfulness nearly broke her heart.

"I guess you can go if you want to."

"Thank you, Ellen."

"I've reckoned it all out," said Carolus. "We can do it for twenty dollars. We ought to get transportation. Somebody ought to make a present to the veterans, the Government ought to, or the trusts, or the railroads."

"Where will we stay?" asked Gunner Cris-

well. His hands trembled suddenly and he
laid down the stiff reeds.

"They'll have places. I bet they'll skin us
for board, though. The minute I get there
I'm going straight to that monument to hunt
for my name. They'll have us all arranged
by regiments and companies. I'll find yours
for you."

The hand of the blind man opened and
closed. He could find his own name, thank
Heaven! he could touch it, could press his
palm upon it, know that it was there, feel
it in his own soul — Adam Criswell. His calm
vanished, his passive philosophy melted in the
heat of old desires relit, desire for fame, for
power, for life. He was excited, discontented,
happy yet unhappy. Such an experience
would crown his life; it would be all the more
wonderful because it had never been dreamed
of. That night he could not sleep. He saw
his name, Adam Criswell, written where it
would stand for generations to come. From
that time on he counted the days, almost the
hours, until he should start for Gettysburg.

Carolus Depew was a selfish person, for

all his apparent devotion to his friend. Having arrived at Gettysburg, he had found the monument, and he had impatiently hunted for the place of Gunner Criswell's Battery B, and guided his hand to the raised letters, and then had left him alone.

"I've found it!" he shouted, a moment later. "'Carolus Depew, Corporal,' big as life. 'Carolus Depew, Corporal'! What do you think of that, say! It'll be here in a hundred years, 'Carolus Depew, Corporal'!"

Then Carolus wandered a little farther along the line of tablets and round to the other side of the great monument. Gunner Criswell called to him lightly, as though measuring the distance he had gone. When Carolus did not answer, Gunner Criswell spoke to a boy who had offered him souvenir postal cards. It was like him to take his joy quietly, intensely.

"Will you read the names of this battery for me?" he asked.

The boy sprang as though he had received a command. It was not only the man's blindness which won men and women and children;

his blindness was seldom apparent; it was his
air of power and strength.

The boy read the list slowly and distinctly,
and then refused the nickel which Criswell
offered him. In a moment Carolus returned,
still thrilled by his own greatness, as excited
as a child.

"We must hunt a place to stay now," he
said. "This is a grand spot. There's monuments as far as the eye can reach. Come on.
Ain't you glad to walk with 'Carolus Depew,
Corporal'?"

It was three o'clock in the afternoon when
Carolus left Gunner Criswell on a doorstep
in Gettysburg and went in search of rooms.
At a quarter to six the blind man still sat on
the same spot. He was seventy years old and
he was tired, and the cold step chilled him
through. He did not dare to move; it seemed
to him that thousands of persons passed and
repassed. If he went away, Carolus could not
find him. And where should he go? He felt
tired and hungry and worn and old; his great
experience of the afternoon neither warmed
nor fed him; he wished himself back in his

own place with his work and his peace of mind and Ellen.

Then, suddenly, he realized that some one was speaking to him. The voice was a woman's, low-pitched, a little imperious, the voice of one not accustomed to be kept waiting.

"Will you please move and let me ring this door-bell?"

Gunner Criswell sprang to his feet. He did not like to acknowledge his infirmity; it seemed always like bidding for sympathy. But now the words rushed from him, words than which there are none more heartrending.

"Madam, forgive me! I am blind."

A perceptible interval passed before the woman answered. Once Gunner Criswell thought she had gone away.

Instead she was staring at him, her heart throbbing. She laid her hand on his arm.

"Why do you sit here on the steps? Have you no place to stay?"

Gunner Criswell told her about Carolus.

"You must come to my house," she invited.

Gunner Criswell explained that he could

not leave his friend. "He would be worried
if he could n't find me. He" — Gunner Criswell turned his head, then he smiled — "he
is coming now. I can hear him."

Protesting, scolding, Carolus came down
the street. He was with several other veterans, and all were complaining bitterly
about the lack of accommodations. The lady
looked at Carolus's untidiness, then back at
the blind man.

"I can take you both," she said. "My name
is Mrs. James, and I live on the college cam-
pus. Anybody can direct you. Tell the maid
I sent you."

Mrs. James's house was large, and in it the
two old men found a comfortable room, distinguished and delightful company, and a
heart-warming dinner. There were five other
guests, who like themselves had neglected to
engage rooms beforehand — a famous general
of the Civil War and four lesser officers. Professor James made them all welcome, and the
two small boys made it plain that this was the
greatest occasion of their lives. The dinner-
table was arranged in a way which Carolus

Depew had never seen; it was lit by candles and decked with the best of the asters from Mrs. James's garden. The officers wore their uniforms, Mrs. James her prettiest dress. Carolus appreciated all the grandeur, but he insisted to the blind man that it was only their due. It was paying a debt which society owed the veteran.

"This professor did n't fight," argued Carolus. "Why should n't he do this for us? They ought n't to charge us a cent. But I bet they will."

Gunner Criswell, refreshed and restored, was wholly grateful. He listened to the pleasant talk, he heard with delight the lovely voice of his hostess, he felt beside him the fresh young body of his hostess's little son. Even the touch of the silver and china pleased him. His wife had brought from her home a few plates as delicate, a few spoons as heavy, and they had had long since to be sold.

Carolus helped the blind man constantly during the meal; he guided his hand to the bread-plate and gave him portions of food, all of which was entirely unnecessary. The blind man was much more deft than Carolus, and the maid was careful and interested and kind. All the guests except the general watched the blind man with admiration. The general talked busily and constantly at the other end of the table; it was not to be expected that he should notice a private soldier.

It was the general who had first proposed inscribing the names of all the soldiers on the great monument; the monument, though he was not a member of the building committee, was his dearest enterprise. Since the war the general had become a statistician; he was interested in lists and tabulations, he enjoyed making due return for value received, he liked to provide pensions, to place old soldiers comfortably in Soldiers' Homes. The war was long past; his memory had begun to grow dim; to his mind the lives of the soldiers would be completed, rounded, by this tribute, as his own would be by the statue of himself which should some day rise upon this field. It was he who had compiled the lists for this last and greatest roster; about it he talked constantly.

Presently, as the guests finished their coffee, one of the lesser officers asked the man next him a question about a charge, and then Professor James asked another, and the war changed suddenly from a thing of statistics and lists and pensions to what it actually was, a thing of horror, of infinite sacrifice, of heroism. Men drilled and marched and fought and suffered and prayed and were slain. The faces of the *raconteurs* glowed, the eager voices of the questioners trembled. Once one of the officers made an effort to draw Gunner Criswell into speech, but Gunner Criswell was shy. He sat with his arm round the little boy, the candle-light shining on his beautiful face, listening with his whole soul. With Carolus it was different. Carolus had several times firmly to be interrupted.

In the morning Mrs. James took the blind man for a drive. The air was as fresh and clear as the air of his own mountains; the little boy sat on a stool between his feet and rested his shoulder against his knee. Mrs. James knew the field thoroughly; she made as plain as possible its topography, the main lines, the great charges, the open fields between the two ridges, the mighty rocks of Devil's Den, the almost impenetrable thickets. To Gunner Criswell, Gettysburg had been a little smoke-o'erlaid town seen faintly at the end of a long march, its recollection dimmed afterward by terrible physical pain. He realized now for the first time the great territory which the battle-lines inclosed, he understood the titanic grandeur of the event of which he had been a part, he breathed in also the present and enduring peace. He touched the old muzzle-loading cannon; the little boy guided his hand to the tiny tombstones in the long lines of graves of the unknown; he stood where Lincoln had stood, weary, heart-sick, despairing, in the fall of '63.

Then, strangely for him, Gunner Criswell began to talk. Something within him seemed to have broken, hidden springs of feeling seemed to well up in his heart. It was the talk of a man at peace with himself, reconciled, happy, conscious of his own value, sure of his place in the scheme of things. He talked as he had never talked in his life — of his youth, of his hopes, of his wife, of Ellen. It was almost more than Mrs. James could endure.

"It is coming back here that makes you feel like this," she said brokenly. "You realize how tremendous it was, and you know that you did your part and that you haven't been forgotten, that you were important in a great cause."

"Yes, ma'am," answered Gunner Criswell, in his old-fashioned way. "It is that exactly."

Mrs. James had little respect for rank as such. She and the great general, the four lesser officers, her husband and her two boys, were to drive together to the dedication that afternoon and to have seats on the platform, and thither she took Private Criswell. Carolus Depew was not sorry to be relieved of the care of the blind man; he had found some old comrades and was crazy with excitement.

"It is a good thing that she invited you," said Carolus, "because we are going to march, just like we used to, and you couldn't very well."

The dedication exercises were not long. To the blind man there was the singing which

HE STOOD WHERE LINCOLN HAD STOOD

stirred his heart, there was the cool air in his face, there was the touch of the little boy's hand, there was Mrs. James's voice in explanation or description.

"There is the Governor!" cried Mrs. James. "He will pass right beside you. There is the Secretary of War. You can hear him talking to the Governor if you listen carefully. That deep voice is his. *Can* you hear?"

"Oh, yes," answered the blind man happily.

He heard the speeches, he heard the music, he could tell by the wild shouting when the great enveloping flag drifted to the ground and the monument stood wholly unveiled; he could feel presently the vast crowd beginning to depart. He stood quietly while the great general near him laughed and talked, receiving the congratulations of great men, presenting the great men to Mrs. James; he heard other bursts of cheering, other songs. He was unspeakably happy.

Then suddenly he felt a strange hand on his arm. The general was close to him, was speaking to him; there was a silence all about them. The general turned him a little as he spoke toward the great bronze tablets with their record of the brave.

"You were in the army?" asked the general.

"Yes, sir."

"In what regiment?"

"I was in Battery B, sir."

"Then," said the general, "let us find your name."

Mrs. James came forward to the blind man's side. The general wished to make visible, actual, the rewarding of the soldier, and she was passionately thankful that it was upon this man that the general's eye had fallen.

But Gunner Criswell, to her astonishment, held back. Then he said an extraordinary thing for one who hesitated always to make his infirmity plain, and for one who could read the raised letters, who had read them, here on this very spot. He said again those three words, only a little less dreadful than the other three terrible words, "He is dead."

"Oh, sir," he cried, "I cannot read! I am blind!"

The general flung his arm across the blind man's shoulder. He was a tall man also, and magnificently made. It gave one a thrill to see them stand together.

"I will read for you."

"But, sir —" Still Gunner Criswell hung back, his hand clutching the little boy's, his beautiful, sightless eyes turned toward Mrs. James, as though he would have given anything to save her, to save any of them, pain. "It is not a question of reward, sir. I would endure it all again, gladly — everything. I don't count it, sir. But do not look for my name. It is chance, accident. It might have happened to any one, sir. It is not your fault. But my name has been omitted."

VI
THE SUBSTITUTE

VI

THE SUBSTITUTE

IT was nine o'clock on the eve of Memorial Day, and pandemonium reigned on the platform of the little railroad station at Gettysburg. A heavy thunderstorm, which had brought down a score of fine trees on the battle-field, and had put entirely out of service the electric light plant of the town, was just over. In five minutes the evening train from Harrisburg would be due, and with it the last delegation to the convention of the Grand Army of the Republic.

A spectator might have thought it doubtful whether the arriving delegation would be able to set foot upon the crowded platform. In the dim light, representatives from the hotels and boarding-houses fought each other for places on the steps beyond which the town council had forbidden them to go. Back of them, along the pavement, their unwatched horses stood patiently, too tired to make even the slight movement which would have inextricably tangled the wheels of the omnibuses and tourist wagons. On the platform were a hundred old soldiers, some of them still hale, others crippled and disabled, and as many women, the "Ladies of the Relief Corps," come to assist in welcoming the strangers. The railroad employees elbowed the crowd good-naturedly, as their duties took them from one part of the station to another; small boys chased each other, racing up the track to catch the first glimpse of the headlight of the train; and presently all joined in a wild and joyous singing of "My Country, 't is of Thee."

High above the turmoil, on a baggage truck which had been pushed against the wall, stood "Old Man Daggett," whistling. He was apparently unaware of the contrast between the whiteness of his beard and the abandoned gayety of his tune, which was "We won't go home until morning"; he was equally unaware or indifferent to the care with which the crowd avoided his neighborhood. But though he had been drinking, he was not drunk. He looked down upon the crowd, upon his former companions in the Grand Army post, who had long since repudiated him because of the depths to which he had fallen; he thought of the days when he had struggled with the other guides for a place at the edge of the platform, and, wretched as was his present condition, he continued to whistle.

When, presently, the small boys shouted, "There she comes!" the old man added his cheer to the rest, purely for the joy of hearing his own voice. The crowd lurched forward, the station agent ordered them back, the engine whistled, her bell rang, the old soldiers called wildly, "Hello, comrades!" "Hurrah, comrades!" and the train stopped. Then ensued a wilder pandemonium. There were multitudinous cries: —

"Here you are, the Keystone House!"

"Here you are, the Palace, the official hotel of Gettysburg!"

"The Battle Hotel, the best in the city!"

There were shouts also from the visitors.

"Hello, comrades! Hurrah! Hurrah!"

"Did you ever see such a storm?"

"Hurrah! Hurrah!"

At first it seemed impossible to bring order out of the chaos. The human particles would rush about forever, wearing themselves into nothingness by futile contact with one another. Presently, however, one of the carriages drove away and then another, and the crowd began to thin. Old Daggett watched them with cheerful interest, rejoicing when Jakie Barsinger of the Palace, or Bert Taylor of the Keystone, lost his place on the steps. By and by his eyes wandered to the other end of the dim platform. Three men stood there, watching the crowd. The sight of three prosperous visitors, unclaimed and unsolicited by the guides, seemed to rouse some latent energy in old Daggett. It was almost ten years since he had guided any one over the field. He scrambled down from the truck and approached the visitors.

"Have you gentlemen engaged rooms?" he asked. "Or a guide?"

The tallest of the three men answered. He was Ellison Brant, former Congressman, of great wealth and vast physical dimensions. His manner was genial and there was a frank cordiality in his voice which his friends admired and his enemies distrusted. His companions, both younger than himself, were two faithful henchmen, Albert Davis and Peter Hayes. They had not heard of the convention in Gettysburg, which they were visiting for the first time, and, irritated by having to travel in the same coach with the noisy veterans, they were now further annoyed by the discovery that all the hotels in the town were crowded. Brant's voice had lost entirely its cordial tone.

"Have you any rooms to recommend?"

"You can't get places at the hotels any more," answered Daggett. "But I could get you rooms."

"Where is your best hotel?"

"Right up here. We'll pass it."

"All right. Take us there first."

Brant's irritation found expression in an oath as they went up the narrow, uneven pavement. He was accustomed to obsequious porters, and his bag was heavy. It was not their guide's age which prevented Brant from giving him the burden, but the fear that he might steal off with it, down a dark alley or side street.

"There's the Keystone," said Daggett. "You can't get in there."

The hotel was brilliantly lighted, a band played in its lobby, and out to the street extended the cheerful, hurrahing crowd. General Davenant, who was to be the orator at the Memorial Day celebration, had come out on a balcony to speak to them. Brant swore again in his disgust.

"I can take you to a fine place," insisted old Daggett.

"Go on, then," said Brant. "What are you waiting for?"

A square farther on, Dagget rapped at the door of a little house. The woman who opened it, lamp in hand, seemed at first unwilling to listen.

"You can't get in here, you old rascal."

But Daggett had put his foot inside the door.

"I've got three fine boarders for you," he

whispered. "You can take 'em or leave 'em. I can take them anywhere and get a quarter apiece for them."

The woman opened the door a little wider and peered out at the three men. Their appearance seemed to satisfy her.

"Come in, comrades," she invited cordially. She had not meant to take boarders during this convention, but these men looked as though they could pay well. "I have fine rooms and good board."

Daggett stepped back to allow the strangers to go into the house.

"I'll be here at eight o'clock sharp to take you over the field, gentlemen," he promised.

There was a briskness about his speech and an alertness in his step, which, coupled with the woman's gratitude, kept her from telling her guests what a reprobate old Daggett was.

By some miracle of persuasion or threat, he secured a two-seated carriage and an ancient horse for the next day's sight-seeing. A great roar of laughter went up from the drivers of the long line of carriages before the Keystone House, as he drove by.

"Where you going to get your passengers, Daggett?"

"Daggett's been to the bone-yard for a horse."

"He ain't as old as your joke," called Daggett cheerfully.

The prospect of having work to do gave him for the moment greater satisfaction than the thought of what he meant to buy with his wages, which was saying a great deal. He began to repeat to himself fragments of his old speech.

"Yonder is the Seminary cupilo objecting above the trees," he said to himself. "From that spot, ladies and gentlemen — from that spot, ladies and gentlemen —" He shook his head and went back to the beginning. "Yonder is the Seminary cupilo. From that spot —" He was a little frightened when he found that he could not remember. "But when I'm there it'll come back," he said to himself.

His three passengers were waiting for him on the steps, while from behind them peered the face of their hostess, curious to see whether old Daggett would keep his word.

Brant looked at the ancient horse with dis-
approval.

"Is everything in this town worn out, like
you and your horse?" he asked roughly.

Dagget straightened his shoulders, which
had not been straightened with pride or re-
sentment for many days.

"You can take me and my horse or you
can leave us," he said.

Brant had already clambered into the carriage. Early in the morning Davis and Hayes
had tried to find another guide, but had failed.

As they drove down the street, the strangers
were aware that every passer-by stopped to
look at them. People glanced casually at the
horse and carriage, as one among a multitude
which had started over the field that morning, then, at sight of the driver, their eyes
widened, and sometimes they grinned. Daggett did not see — he was too much occupied
in trying to remember his speech. The three
men had lighted long black cigars, and were
talking among themselves. The cool morning
air which blew into their faces from the west
seemed to restore Brant's equanimity, and

he offered Daggett a cigar, which Daggett took and put into his pocket. Daggett's lips were moving, he struggled desperately to remember. Presently his eyes brightened.

"Ah!" he said softly. Then he began his speech: —

"Yonder is the Seminary cupilo objecting above the trees. From there Buford observed the enemy, from there the eagle eye of Reynolds took in the situation at a glance, from there he decided that the heights of Gettysburg was the place to fight. You will see that it is an important strategic point, an important strategic point" — his lips delighted in the long-forgotten words. "And here —"

The old horse had climbed the hill, and they were upon the Confederate battle-line of the third day's fight. Old Daggett's voice was lost for an instant in a recollection of his ancient oratorical glories. His speech had been learned from a guide-book, but there was a time when it had been part of his soul.

"Here two hundred cannons opened fire, ladies and gentlemen. From the Union side nearly a hundred guns replied, not because

we had no more guns, ladies and gentlemen,
but, owing to the contour of the ground, we
could only get that many in position at one
time. Then came the greatest artillery duel
of the war — nearly three hundred cannons
bleaching forth their deadly measles, shells
bursting and screaming everywhere. The
shrieks of the dying and wounded were
mingled with the roar of the iron storm. The
earth trembled for hours. It was fearful,
ladies and gentlemen, fearful."

The visitors had been too deeply interested
in what they were saying to hear.

"You said we were on the Confederate
battle-line?" asked Brant absently.

"The Confederate battle-line," answered
Daggett.

He had turned the horse's head toward
Round Top, and he did not care whether they
heard or not.

"Yonder in the distance is Round Top; to
the left is Little Round Top. They are important strategic points. There the Unionists
were attackted in force by the enemy. There
— but here as we go by, notice the breech-

loading guns to our right. They were rare. Most of the guns were muzzle-loaders."

Presently the visitors began to look about them. They said the field was larger than they expected; they asked whether the avenues had been there at the time of the battle; they asked whether Sherman fought at Gettysburg.

"Sherman!" said Daggett. "Here? No." He looked at them in scorn. "But here" — the old horse had stopped without a signal — "here is where Pickett's charge started."

He stepped down from the carriage into the dusty road. This story he could not tell as he sat at ease. He must have room to wave his arms, to point his whip.

"They aimed toward that clump of trees, a mile away. They marched with steady step, as though they were on dress parade. When they were half way across the Union guns began to fire. They was torn apart; the rebel comrades stepped over the dead and went on through the storm of deadly measles as though it was rain and wind. When they started they was fifteen thousand; when they got back they was eight. They was almost annihilated. You could walk from the stone wall to beyond the Emmitsburg road without treading on the ground, the bodies lay so thick. Pickett and his men had done their best."

"Well done!" cried Brant, when he was through. "Now, that'll do. We want to talk. Just tell us when we get to the next important place."

They drove on down the wide avenue. Spring had been late, and there were lingering blossoms of dogwood and Judas-tree. Here and there a scarlet tanager flashed among the leaves; rabbits looked brightly at them from the wayside, and deep in the woods resounded the limpid note of a wood-robin.

Disobedient to Brant's command, Daggett was still talking, repeating to himself all the true and false statements of his old speeches. Some, indeed, were mad absurdities.

"There's only one Confederate monument on the field," he said. "You can tell it when we get there. It says 'C. S. A.' on it — 'Secesh Soldiers of America.'

"There was great fightin' round Spangler's Spring," he went on soberly. "There those that had no legs gave water to those that had no arms, and those that had no arms carried off those that had no legs."

At the summit of Little Round Top the old horse stopped again.

"You see before you the important strategic points of the second day's fight —Devil's Den, the Wheat-Field, the Valley of Death. Yonder —"

Suddenly the old man's memory seemed to fail. He whispered incoherently, then he asked them if they wanted to get out.

"No," said Brant.

"But everybody gets out here," insisted Daggett peevishly. "You can't see Devil's Den unless you do. You *must* get out."

"All right," acquiesced Brant. "Perhaps we are not getting our money's worth."

He lifted himself ponderously down, and Davis followed him.

"I'll stay here," said Hayes. "I'll see that our driver don't run off. Were you a soldier?" he asked the old man.

"Yes," answered Daggett. "I was wounded in this battle. I was n't old enough to go, but they took me as a substitute for another man. And I never" — an insane anger flared in the old man's eyes — "I never got my bounty. He was to have paid me a thousand dollars. A thousand dollars!" He repeated it as though the sum were beyond his computation. "After I came out I was going to set up in business. But the skunk never paid me."

"What did you do afterwards?"

"Nothing," said Daggett. "I was wounded here, and I stayed here after I got well, and hauled people round. Hauled people round!" He spoke as though the work were valueless, degrading.

"Why did n't you go into business?"

"I did n't have my thousand dollars," replied Daggett petulantly. "Did n't I tell you I did n't have my thousand dollars? The skunk never paid me."

The thought of the thousand dollars of which he had been cheated seemed to paralyze the old man. He told them no more stories; he drove silently past Stannard, high on his

great shaft, Meade on his noble horse, front-
ing the west. He did not mention Stubborn
Smith or gallant Armistead. Brant, now that
he had settled with his friends some legisla-
tive appointments which he controlled, was
ready to listen, and was angry at the old man's
silence.

"When you take us back to town, you take
us to that hotel we saw last night," he ordered.
"We're not going back to your lady friend."

Old Daggett laughed. Lady friend! How
she would scold! He would tell her that the
gentlemen thought she was his lady friend.

"And we'll have to have a better horse and
driver after dinner, if we're going to see this
field."

"All right," said Daggett.

His morning's work would buy him drink
for a week, and beyond the week he had no
interest.

He drove the ancient horse to the hotel,
and his passengers got out. He waited, ex-
pecting to be sent for their baggage. The porch
and pavement were as crowded as they had
been the night before. The soldiers embraced

each other, hawkers cried their picture post-cards and their manufactured souvenirs, at the edge of the pavement a band was play-ing.

Brant pushed his way to the clerk's desk. The clerk remembered him at once as the triumphantly vindicated defendant in a Congressional scandal, and welcomed him obsequiously. Brant's picture had been in all the papers, and his face was not easily forgotten.

"Well, sir, did you just get in?" the clerk asked politely.

"No, I've been here all night," answered Brant. "I was told you had no rooms."

Meanwhile old Daggett had become tired of waiting. He wanted his money; the Keystone people might send for the baggage. He tied his old horse, unheeding the grins of his former companions in the army post and of the colored porters and the smiles of the fine ladies. He followed Brant into the hotel.

"Who said we had n't rooms?" he heard the clerk say to Brant, and then he heard Brant's reply: "An old drunk."

"Old Daggett?" said the clerk.

A frown crossed Brant's handsome face. "Daggett?" he repeated sharply. "Frederick Daggett?"

Then he looked back over his shoulder.

"Yes, Frederick Daggett," said the old man himself. "What of it?"

"Nothing," answered Brant nervously.

He pulled out his purse and began to pay the old man, aware that the crowd had turned to listen.

But the old man did not see the extended hand. He was staring at Brant's smooth face as though he saw it for the first time.

"You pay me my money," he said thickly.

"I am paying you your money," answered Brant.

The clerk looked up, meaning to order old Daggett out. Then his pen dropped from his hand as he saw Brant's face.

"You give me my thousand dollars," said Daggett. "I want my thousand dollars."

Some one in the crowd laughed. Every one in Gettysburg had heard of Daggett's thousand dollars.

"Put him out! He's crazy."

"Be still," said some one, who was watching Brant.

"I want my thousand dollars," said old Daggett, again. He looked as though, even in his age and weakness, he would spring upon Brant. "I want my thousand dollars."

Brant thrust a trembling hand into his pocket and drew out his check-book. If he had had a moment to think, if the face before him had not been so ferocious, if General Davenant, whom he knew, and who knew him, had not been looking with stern inquiry over old Daggett's shoulder, he might have laughed, or he might have pretended that he had tried to find Daggett after the war, or he might have denied that he had ever seen him. But before he thought of an expedient, it was too late. He had committed the fatal blunder of drawing out his check-book.

"Be quiet and I'll give it to you," he said, beginning to write.

Daggett almost tore the slip of blue paper from his hand.

"I won't be quiet!" he shouted, in his weak voice, hoarse from his long speech in the morning. "This is the man that got me to substitute for him and cheated me out of my thousand dollars. I won't be quiet!" He looked down at the slip of paper in his hand. Perhaps it was the ease with which Brant paid out such a vast sum that moved him, perhaps it was the uselessness of the thousand dollars, now that he was old. He tore the blue strip across and threw it on the floor. "There is your thousand dollars!"

He had never looked so wretchedly miserable as he did now. He was ragged and dusty, and the copious tears of age were running down his cheeks. His were not the only tears in the crowd. A member of his old post, which had repudiated him, seized him by the arm.

"Come with me, Daggett. We'll fix you up. We'll make it up to you, Daggett."

But Daggett jerked away.

"Get out. I'll fix myself up if there's any fixing."

He walked past Brant, not deigning to look at him, he stepped upon the fragments of paper on the floor, and shambled to the door. There he saw the faces of Jakie Barsinger and

Bert Taylor and the other guides who had laughed at him, who had called him "Thousand-Dollar" Daggett, now gaping at him. Old Daggett's cheerfulness returned.

"You blame' fools could n't earn a thousand dollars if you worked a thousand years. And I" — he waved a scornful hand over his shoulder — "I can throw a thousand dollars away."

VII

THE RETREAT

VII

THE RETREAT

GRANDFATHER MYERS rose stiffly from his knees. He had been weeding Henrietta's nasturtium bed, which, thanks to him, was always the finest in the neighborhood of Gettysburg. As yet, the plants were not more than three inches high, and the old man tended them as carefully as though they were children. He was thankful now that his morning's work was done, the wood-box filled, the children escorted part of the way to school, and the nasturtium bed weeded, for he saw the buggy of the mail-carrier of Route 4 come slowly down the hill. It was grandfather's privilege to bring the mail in from the box. This time he reached it before the postman, and waited smilingly for him. It always reminded him a little of his youth, when the old stone house behind him had been a tavern, and the stage drew up before it each morning with flourish of horn and proud curveting of horses.

The postman waved something white at him as he approached.

"Great news for Gettysburg," he called. "The state militia's coming to camp in July."

"You don't say so!" exclaimed Grandfather Myers.

"Yes, they'll be here a week."

"How many'll there be?"

"About ten thousand."

Grandfather started away in such excitement that the postman had to call him back to receive the newspaper. The old man took it and hobbled up the yard, his trembling hands scarcely able to unfold it. He paused twice to read a paragraph, and when he reached the porch he sat down on the upper step, the paper quivering in his hands.

"Henrietta!" he called.

His son's wife appeared in the doorway, a large, strong, young woman with snapping eyes. She was drying a platter and her arms moved vigorously.

"What is it, grandfather?" she asked impatiently.

The old man was so excited he could scarcely answer.

"There's going to be an encampment at Gettysburg, Henrietta. All the state troops is going to be here. It'll be like war-time again. It says here —"

"I like to read the paper my own self, father," said Henrietta, moving briskly away from the door. She felt a sudden anger that it was grandfather who had this great piece of news to tell. "You ain't taken your weeds away from the grass yet, and it's most dinner-time."

Grandfather laid down the paper and went to finish his task. He was accustomed to Henrietta's surliness, and nothing made him unhappy very long. He threw the weeds over the fence and then went back to the porch. So willing was he to forgive Henrietta, and so anxious to tell her more of the exciting news in the paper, that, sitting on the steps, he read her extracts.

"Ten thousand of 'em, Henrietta. They're

going to camp around Pickett's Charge, and near the Codori Farm, and they're going to put the cavalry and artillery near Reynolds Woods, and some regulars are coming, Henrietta. It'll be like war-time. And they're going to have a grand review with the soldiers marchin' before the Governor. The Governor'll be there, Henrietta! And —"

"I don't believe it's true," remarked Henrietta coldly. "I believe it's just newspaper talk."

"Oh, no, Henrietta!" Grandfather spoke with deep conviction. "There would n't be no cheatin' about such a big thing as this. The Government'd settle them if they'd publish lies. And —" grandfather rose in his excitement — "there'll be cannons a-boomin' and guns a-firin' and oh, my!" He waved the paper above his head. "And the review! I guess you ain't ever seen so many men together. But I have. I tell you I have. When I laid upstairs here, with the bullet in here" — he laid his hand upon his chest — "I seen 'em goin'." Grandfather's voice choked as the voice of one who speaks of some tremendous experience of his past. "I seen 'em goin'. Men and men and men and horses and horses and wagons. They was millions, Henrietta."

Henrietta did not answer. She said to herself that she had heard the account of grandfather's millions of men millions of times. Wounded at Chancellorsville, and sent home on furlough, he had watched the Confederate retreat from an upper window of the old stone house.

"I woke up in the night, and I looked out," he would say. "Everybody was sleepin' and I crept over to the window. It was raining like" — here grandfather's long list of comparisons failed, and he described it simply — "it was just rain and storm and marchin'. They kept going and going. It was tramp, tramp all night."

"Did n't anybody speak, grandfather?" the children would ask.

"You could n't hear 'em for the rain," he would answer. "Once in a while you could hear 'em cryin'. But most of the time it was just rain and storm, rain and storm. They could n't go fast, they —"

"Why did n't our boys catch them?" little Caleb always asked. "I 'd 'a' run after them."

"Our boys was tired." Grandfather dismissed the Union army with one short sentence. "The rebels kept droppin' in their tracks. There was two dead front of the porch in the morning, and three across the bridge. I tried to sneak out in the night and give 'em something to eat, or ask some of 'em to come in, but the folks said I was too sick. They would n't let me go. I—"

"It would 'a' been a nice thing to help the enemies of your country that you 'd been fightin' against!" Henrietta would sometimes say scornfully.

"You did n't see 'em marchin' and hear the sick ones cryin' when the rain held up a little," he reminded Henrietta. "Oh, I wish I 'd sneaked out and done something for 'em!"

Then he would lapse into silence, his eyes on the long, red road which led to Hagerstown. It lay now clear and hot and treeless in the sunshine; to his vision, however, the dust was whipped into deep mud by a beating rain, beneath which Lee and his army "marched and marched." He leaned forward as though straining to see.

"I saw some flags once when it lightened," he said; "and once I thought I saw General Lee."

"Oh, I guess not!" Henrietta would answer with scornful indulgence to which grandfather was deaf.

He read the newspaper announcement of the encampment again and again, then he went to meet the children on their way from school, stopping to tell their father, who was at work in the field.

"There'll be a grand review," grandfather said. "Ten thousand soldiers in line. We'll go to it, John. It'll be a great day for the young ones."

"We'll see," answered John.

He was a brisk, energetic man, too busy to be always patient.

In the children grandfather had his first attentive listeners.

"Will it be like the war?" they asked, eagerly.

"Oh, something. There won't be near so many, and they won't kill nobody. But it'll be a great time. They'll drill all day long."

"Will their horses' hoofs sound like dry leaves rustlin'?" asked little Mary, who always remembered most clearly what the old man had said.

"Yes, like leaves a-rustlin'," repeated the old man. "You must be good children, now, so you don't miss the grand review."

All through the early summer they talked of the encampment. Because of it the annual Memorial Day visit to the battle-field was omitted. Each night the children heard the story of the battle and the retreat, until they listened for commands, faintly given, and the sound of thousands of weary feet. Grandfather often got up in the night and looked out across the yard to the road. Sometimes they heard him whispering to himself as he went back to bed. He got down his old sword and spent many hours trying to polish away the rust which had been gathering for forty years.

"You expect to wear the sword, father?" asked Henrietta, laughing.

News of the encampment reached them constantly. Three weeks before it opened, they were visited by a man who wished to hire horses for the use of the cavalry and the artillery. John debated for a moment. The wheat was in, the oats could wait until the encampment was over, the price paid for horse hire was good. He told the man that he might have Dick, one of the heavy draft horses.

Grandfather ran to meet the children as they came from a neighbor's.

"Dick's going to the war," he cried excitedly.

"To the war?" repeated the children.

"I mean to the encampment. He's been hired. He's going to help pull one of the cannons for the artill'ry."

The next week John drove into town with a load of early apples. He was offered work at a dozen different places. Supplies were being sent in, details of soldiers were beginning to lay out the camp and put up tents, Gettysburg was already crowded with visitors.

Grandfather made him tell it all the second time; then he explained the formation of an army to the children.

"First comes a company, that's the smallest, then a regiment, then a brigade. A quartermaster looks after supplies, a sutler is a fellow who sells things to the soldiers. But, children, you should 'a' seen 'em marching by that night!" Grandfather always came back to the retreat. "They had n't any sutlers to sell 'em anything to eat. I wish — I wish I'd sneaked out and given 'em something."

After grandfather went upstairs that night he realized that he was thirsty, and he came down again. The children were asleep, but their father and mother still sat talking on the porch. Grandfather had taken off his shoes and came upon them before they were aware.

"I don't see no use in his going," Henrietta was saying. "There ain't no room for him in the buggy with us and the children. Where'd we put him? And he saw the real war."

"But he's looked forward to it, Henrietta, he —"

"Well, would you have me stay at home, or would you have the children stay at home, or what?" Henrietta felt the burden of Grandfather Myers more every day. "He'll forget it anyhow in a few days. He forgets everything."

"Do you — do you —" They turned to see grandfather behind them. He held weakly to the side of the door. "Do you mean I ain't to go, Henrietta?"

It did not occur to him to appeal to his son.

"I don't see how you can," answered Henrietta. She was sorry he had heard. She meant to have John tell him gently the next day. "There is only the buggy, and if John goes and I and the children — it's you have made them so anxious to go."

She spoke as though she blamed him.

"But —" Grandfather ignored the meanness of the excuse. "But could n't we take the wagon?"

"The wagon? To Gettysburg? With the whole country looking on? I guess they'd think John was getting along fine if we went in the wagon." Henrietta was glad to have

so foolish a speech to answer as it deserved.
"Why, grandfather!"

"Then" — grandfather's brain, which had
of late moved more and more slowly, was
suddenly quickened — "then let me drive the
wagon and you can go in the buggy. I can
drive Harry and nobody'll know I belong to
you, and —"

"Let you drive round with all them
horses and the shooting and everything!"
exclaimed Henrietta.

Her husband turned toward her.

"You might drive the buggy and take
grandfather, and I could go in the wagon,"
he said.

"I don't go to Gettysburg without a man
on such a day," said Henrietta firmly.

"But —" Grandfather interrupted his own
sentence with a quavering laugh. Henrietta
did not consider him a man!

Then he turned and went upstairs, forgetting his drink of water. He heard Henrietta's
voice long afterward, and John's low answers.
John wanted him to go, he did not blame
John.

The next day he made a final plea. He followed John to the barn.

"Seems as if I might ride Harry," he said tentatively.

"O father, you could n't," John answered gently. "You know how it will be, noise and confusion and excitement. Harry is n't used to it. You could n't manage him."

"Seems as though if Dick goes, Harry ought to go, too. 'T ain't fair for Dick to go, and not Harry," he whispered childishly.

"I'm sorry, father," said John.

It was better that his father should be disappointed than that Henrietta should be opposed. His father would forget in a few days and Henrietta would remember for weeks.

The next day when the man came for Dick they found grandfather in the stable patting the horse and talking about the war. He watched Dick out of sight, and then sat down in his armchair on the porch whispering to himself.

The children protested vigorously when they found that the old man was not going, but they were soon silenced by their mother.

Grandfather was old, it was much better that he should not go.

"You can tell him all about it when you come home," she said.

"You can guard the place while we're gone, Grandfather," suggested little Caleb. "Perhaps the Confederates will come back."

"They wouldn't hurt nothing," answered the old man. "They was tired — tired — tired."

When the family drove away he sat on the porch. He waved his hand until he could see little Mary's fluttering handkerchief no more, then he fell asleep. As Henrietta said, he soon forgot. When he woke up a little later, he went down to the barn and patted Harry, then he went out to the mail-box to see whether by any chance he had missed a letter. He looked at the nasturtium bed, now aglow with yellow and orange and deep crimson blossoms, then he went back to the porch. He was lonely. He missed the sound of John's voice calling to the horses down in the south meadow or across the road in the wheat-field, he missed the chatter of the children, he missed even their mother's curt answers to his questions. For an instant he wondered where they had gone, then he sighed heavily as he remembered. Instead of sitting down again in his chair, he went into the house and upstairs. There he tiptoed warily up to the garret as if he were afraid that some one would follow him, and drew from a hiding-place which he fancied no one knew but himself an old coat, blue, with buttons of dull, tarnished brass. He thrust his arms into it, still whispering to himself, and smoothed it down. His fingers hesitated as they touched a jagged rent just in front of the shoulder.

"What — Oh, yes, I remember!"

Grandfather had never been quite so forgetful as this. On his way downstairs he took from its hook his old sword.

"Caleb says I must guard the house," he said smilingly.

When he reached the porch, he turned his chair so that it no longer faced toward Gettysburg, whither John and Henrietta and the children had gone, but toward the blue hills and Hagerstown. Once he picked up the sword and pointed with it, steadying it with both hands. "Through that gap they went," he said.

Then he dozed again. The old clock, which had stood on the kitchen mantelpiece since before he was born, struck ten, but he did not hear. Henrietta had told him where he could find some lunch, but he did not remember nor care. His dinner was set out beneath a white cloth on the kitchen table, but he had not curiosity enough to lift it and see what good things Henrietta had left for him. When he woke again, he began to sing in a shrill voice: —

> "Away down South in Dixie,
>   Look away, look away."

"They did n't sing that when they was marching home," he said solemnly. "They only tramped along in the dark and rain."

Then suddenly he straightened up. Like an echo from his own lips, there came from the distance toward Gettysburg the same tune, played by fifes, with the dull accompaniment of drums. He bent forward, listening, then stood up, looking off toward the blue hills. At once he realized that the sound came from the other direction.

"I thought they was all past, long ago," he said. "And they never played. I guess I was asleep and dreaming."

He sat down once more, his head on his breast. When he lifted it, it was in response to a sharp "Halt!" He stared about him. The road before him was filled with soldiers, in dusty yellow uniforms. Then he was not dreaming, then — He tottered to the edge of the porch.

The men of the Third Regiment of the National Guard of Pennsylvania did not approve of the march, in their parlance a "hike," which their colonel had decided to give them along the line of Lee's retreat. They felt that just before the grand review in the afternoon, it was an imposition. They were glad to halt, while the captain of each company explained that upon the night of the third of July, 1863, Lee had traversed this road on his way to recross the Potomac.

When his explanation was over, the captain of Company I moved his men a little to the right under the shade of the maples. From there he saw the moving figure behind the vines.

"Sergeant, go in and ask whether we may have water."

The sergeant entered the gate, and the thirsty men, hearing the order, looked after him. They saw the strange old figure on the porch, the torn blue jacket belted at the waist, the sword, the smiling, eager face. The captain saw, too.

"Three cheers for the old soldier," he cried, and hats were swung in the air.

"May we have a drink?" the sergeant asked, and grandfather pointed the way to the well.

He tried to go down the steps to help them pump, but his knees trembled, and he stayed where he was. He watched them, still smiling. He did not realize that the cheers were for him, he could not quite understand why suits which should be gray were so yellow, but he supposed it was the mud.

"Poor chaps," he sighed. "They're goin' back to Dixie."

THEY SAW THE STRANGE OLD FIGURE ON THE PORCH

One by one the companies drew up before the gate, and one by one they cheered. They had been cheering ever since the beginning of the encampment — for Meade, for Hancock, for Reynolds, among the dead; for the Governor, the colonel, the leader of the regiment band, among the living. They had enlisted for a good time, for a trip to Gettysburg, for a taste of camp-life, from almost any other motive than that which had moved this old man to enlist in '61. They suddenly realized how little this encampment was like war. All the drill, all the pomp of this tin soldiering, even all the graves of the battlefield, had not moved them as did this old man in his tattered coat. Here was love of country. Would any of them care to don in fifty years their khaki blouses? Then, before the momentary enthusiasm or the momentary seriousness had time to wear away, the order was given to march back to camp.

The old man did not turn to watch them go. He sat still with his eyes upon the distant hills. After a while his sword fell clattering to the floor.

"I'm glad I sneaked out and gave 'em something," he said, smiling with a great content.

The long leaves of the corn in the next field rustled in the wind, the sun rose higher, then declined, and still he sat there smilingly un-heeding, his eyes toward the west. Once he said, "Poor chaps, it's dark for 'em."

The cows waited at the pasture gate for the master and mistress, who were late. Henrietta had wished that morning that grandfather could milk, so that they would not have to hurry home. Presently they came, tired and hungry, the children eager to tell of the wonders they had seen. At their mother's command, they ran to let down the pasture bars while their father led the horses to the barn, and she herself went on to the porch.

"Grandfather," she said kindly, "we're here." She even laid her hand on his shoulder. "Wake up, grandfather!" She spoke sharply, angry at his failure to respond to her unaccustomed gentleness of speech. Her hand fell upon his shoulder once more, this time heavily, and her finger-tips touched a jagged edge of cloth. "What —" she began. She remembered the old coat, which she had long since made up her mind to burn. She felt for the buttons down the front, the belt with its broad plate. Yes, it was — Then suddenly she touched his hands, and screamed and ran, crying, toward the barn.

"John!" she called. "John! Grandfather is dead."

VIII

THE GREAT DAY

VIII

THE GREAT DAY

OLD BILLY GUDE strode slowly into the kitchen, where his wife bent over the stove. Just inside the door he stopped, and chewed meditatively upon the toothpick in his mouth. His wife turned presently to look at him.

"What are you grinning at?" she asked pleasantly.

Billy did not answer. Instead he sat down in his armchair and lifted his feet to the window-sill.

"*Won't* you speak, or can't you?" demanded Mrs. Gude.

When he still did not respond, she gravely pushed her frying-pan to the back of the stove, and went toward the door. Before her hand touched the latch, however, Billy came to himself.

"Abbie!" he cried.

"I can't stop now," answered Mrs. Gude.
"I gave you your chance to tell what you
got to tell. Now you can wait till I come
home."

"You'll be sorry."

Mrs. Gude looked back. Her husband still
grinned.

"You're crazy," she said, with conviction,
and went out.

An instant later she reopened the door.
Billy was executing a *pas seul* in the middle
of the floor.

"*Are* you crazy?" she demanded, in af-
fright.

Billy paused long enough to wink at her.

"You better go do your errand, Abbie."

Abbie seized him by the arm.

"What is the matter?"

Then Billy's news refused longer to be re-
tained.

"There's a great day comin'," he an-
nounced solemnly. "The President of the
United States is comin' here on Decoration
Day to see the battle-field."

"What of that?" said Abbie scornfully.

"It won't do you no good. He'll come in the morning in an automobile, an' he'll scoot round the field with Jakie Barsinger a-settin' on the step tellin' lies, an' you can see him go by."

"See him go by nothin'," declared Billy. "That's where you're left. He's comin' in the mornin' on a special train, an' he's goin' to be driven round the field, an' he's goin' to make a speech at the nostrum" — thus did Billy choose to pronounce rostrum — "an'—"

"And Jakie Barsinger will drive him over the field and to the nostrum, and you can sit and look on."

"That's where you're left again," mocked Billy. "I, bein' the oldest guide, an' the best knowed, an' havin' held Mr. Lincoln by the hand in '63, an' havin' driven all the other big guns what come here till automobiles an' Jakie Barsinger come in, *I* am selected to do the drivin' on the great day."

Mrs. Gude sat down heavily on a chair near the door.

"Who done it, Billy?"

"I don't know who done it," Billy an-

swered. "An' I don't care. Some of the ga-
loots had a little common sense for once."

"*Why* did they do it?" gasped Mrs. Gude.

"Why?" repeated Billy.   "Why?   Because when you get people to talk about a
battle, it's better to have some one what
saw the battle, an' not some one what was
in long clothes. I guess they were afraid Jakie
might tell something wrong. You can't fool
this President."

"I mean, what made 'em change *now?*"
went on Abbie. "They knew this long time
that Jakie Barsinger was dumb."

"I don't know, an' I don't care. I only
know that I'm goin' to drive the President.
I heard Lincoln make his speech in '63, an' I
drove Everett an' Sickles an' Howard an'
Curtin, and this President's father, an' then"
— Billy's voice shook — "then they said I was
gettin' old, an' Jakie Barsinger an' all the
chaps get down at the station an' yell an' howl
like Piute Indians, an' they get the custom,
an' the hotels tell the people I had an accident with an automobile. Automobiles be
danged!"

Mrs. Gude laid a tender hand on his shoulder.

"Don't you cry," she said.

Billy dashed the tears from his eyes.

"I ain't cryin'. You go on with your errand."

Mrs. Gude put on her sunbonnet again. She had no errand, but it would not do to admit it.

"Not if you're goin' to hop round like a loony."

"I'm safe for to-day, I guess. Besides, my legs is give out."

Left alone, Billy rubbed one leg, then the other.

"G'lang there," he said, presently, his hands lifting a pair of imaginary reins. "Mr. President, hidden here among the trees an' bushes waited the foe; here —"

Before he had finished he was asleep. He was almost seventy years old, and excitement wearied him.

For forty years he had shown visitors over the battle-field. At first his old horse had picked his way carefully along lanes and across fields; of late, however, his handsome grays had trotted over fine avenues. The horses knew the route of travel as thoroughly as did their master. They drew up before the National Monument, on the turn of the Angle, and at the summit of Little Round Top without the least guidance.

"There ain't a stone or a bush I don't know," boasted Billy, "there ain't a tree or a fence-post."

Presently, however, came a creature which neither Billy nor his horses knew. It dashed upon them one day with infernal tooting on the steep curve of Culp's Hill, and neither they nor Billy were prepared. He sat easily in his seat, the lines loose in his hands, while he described the charge of the Louisiana Tigers.

"From yonder they came," he said. "Up there, a-creepin' through the bushes, an' then a-dashin', an' down on 'em came —"

And then Billy knew no more. The automobile was upon them; there was a crash as the horses whirled aside into the underbrush, another as the carriage turned turtle, then a

succession of shrieks. No one was seriously
hurt, however, but Billy himself. When,
weeks later, he went back to his old post beside the station platform, where the guides
waited the arrival of trains, Jakie Barsinger
had his place, and Jakie would not move.
He was of a new generation of guides, who
made up in volubility what they lacked in
knowledge.

For weeks Billy continued to drive to the
station. He had enlisted the services of a
chauffeur, and his horses were now accustomed to automobiles.

"I tamed 'em," he said to Abbie. "I drove
'em up to it, an' round it, an' past it. An' he
snorted it, an' tooted it, an' brought it at
'em in front an' behind. They're as calm as
pigeons."

Nevertheless, trade did not come back.
Jakie Barsinger had become the recognized
guide for the guests at the Palace, and John
Harris for those at the Keystone, and it was
always from the hotels that the best patron-
age came.

"Jakie Barsinger took the Secretary of

War round the other day," the old man would say, tearfully, to his wife, "an' he made a fool of himself. He don't know a brigade from a company. An' he grinned at me — he grinned at me!"

Abbie did her best to comfort him.

"Perhaps some of the old ones what used to have you will come back."

"An' if they do," said Billy, "the clerk at the Palace'll tell 'em I ain't in the business, or I was in a accident, or that I'm dead. I wouldn't put it past 'em to tell 'em I'm dead."

Robbed of the occupation of his life, which was also his passion, Billy grew rapidly old. Abbie listened in distress as, sitting alone, he declaimed his old speeches.

"Here on the right they fought with clubbed muskets. Here —"

Often he did not finish, but dozed wearily off. There were times when it seemed that he could not long survive.

Now, however, as Memorial Day approached, he seemed to have taken a new lease of life. No longer did he sit sleepily all

day on the porch or by the stove. He began
to frequent his old haunts, and he assumed
his old proud attitude towards his rivals.

Mrs. Gude did not share his unqualified
elation.

"Something might happen," she suggested
fearfully.

"Nothin' could happen," rejoined Billy
scornfully, "unless I died. An' then I wouldn't
care. But I hope the Lord won't let me die."
Billy said it as though it were a prayer. "I'm
goin' to set up once more an' wave my whip
at 'em, with the President of the United States
beside me. No back seat for him! Colonel
Mott said the President 'd want to sit on the
front seat. An' he said he'd ask questions.
'Let him ask,' I said. 'I ain't afraid of no
questions nobody can ask. No s'tistics, nor
manœuvres, nor —'"

"But Jakie Barsinger might do you a mean
trick."

"There ain't nothin' he *can* do. Mott said
to me, 'Be on time, Gude, bright an' early.'"
Then Billy's voice sank to a whisper. "They're
goin' to stop the train out at the sidin' back

of the Seminary, so as to fool the crowd. They'll be waitin' in town, an' we'll be off an' away. An' by an' by we'll meet Jakie with a load of jays. Oh, it'll be — it'll be immense!"

Through the weeks that intervened before the thirtieth of May, Abbie watched him anxiously. Each day he exercised the horses, grown fat and lazy; each day he went over the long account of the battle, — as though he could forget what was part and parcel of himself! His eyes grew brighter, and there was a flush on his old cheeks. The committee of arrangements lost their fear that they had been unwise in appointing him.

"Gude's just as good as he ever was," said Colonel Mott. "It would n't do to let the President get at Barsinger. If you stop him in the middle of a speech, he has to go back to the beginning." Then he told a story of which he never grew weary. "'Here on this field lay ten thousand dead men,' says Barsinger. 'Ten thousand dead men, interspersed with one dead lady.' No; Billy Gude's all right."

Colonel Mott sighed with relief. The planning for a President's visit was no light task. There were arrangements to be made with the railroad companies, the secret service men were to be stationed over the battle-field, there were to be trustworthy guards, a programme was to be made out for the afternoon meeting at which the President was to speak.

The night before the thirtieth Abbie did not sleep. She heard Billy talking softly to himself.

"Right yonder, Mr. President, they came creepin' through the bushes; right yonder —" Then he groaned heavily, and Abbie shook him awake.

"I was dreamin' about the automobile," he said, confusedly. "I — oh, ain't it time to get up?"

At daylight he was astir, and Abbie helped him dress. His hand shook and his voice trembled as he said good-bye.

"You better come to the window an' see me go past," he said; then, "What you cryin' about, Abbie?"

"I'm afraid somethin' 's goin' to happen," sobbed the old woman. "I'm afraid —"

"Afraid!" he mocked. "Do you think, too, that I'm old an' wore out an' no good? You'll see!"

And, defiantly, he went out.

Half an hour later he drove to the siding where the train was to stop. A wooden platform had been built beside the track, and on it stood Colonel Mott and the rest of the committee.

"Drive back there, Billy," Colonel Mott commanded. "Then when I signal to you, you come down here. And hold on to your horses. There's going to be a Presidential salute. As soon as that's over we'll start."

Billy drew back to the side of the road. Evidently, through some mischance, the plans for the President's reception had become known, and there was a rapidly increasing crowd. On the slope of the hill a battery of artillery awaited the word to fire. Billy sat straight, his eyes on his horses' heads, his old hands gripping the lines. He watched with pride the marshal waving all carriages back from the road. Only he, Billy Gude, had the right to be there. *He* was to drive the President. The great day had come. He chuckled aloud, not noticing that just back of the marshal stood Jakie Barsinger's fine new carriage, empty save for Jakie himself.

Presently the old man sat still more erectly. He heard, clear above the noise of the crowd, a distant whistle — that same whistle for which he had listened daily when he had the best place beside the station platform. The train was rounding the last curve. In a moment more it would come slowly to view out of the fatal Railroad Cut, whose forty-year-old horrors Billy could describe so well.

The fields were black now with the crowd, the gunners watched their captain, and slowly the train drew in beside the bright pine platform. At the door of the last car appeared a tall and sturdy figure, and ten thousand huzzas made the hills ring. Then a thunder of guns awoke echoes which, like the terror-stricken cries from the Railroad Cut, had been silent forty years. Billy, listening, shivered. The horror had not grown less with his repeated telling.

He leaned forward now, watching for

Colonel Mott's uplifted hand; he saw him signal, and then — From behind he heard a cry, and turned to look; then he swiftly swung Dan and Bess in toward the fence. A pair of horses, maddened by the noise of the firing, dashed toward him. He heard women scream, and thought, despairing, of Abbie's prophecy. There would not be room for them to pass. After all, he would not drive the President. Then he almost sobbed in his relief. They were safely by. He laughed grimly. It was Jakie Barsinger with his fine new carriage. Then Billy clutched the reins again. In the short glimpse he had caught of Jakie Barsinger, Jakie did not seem frightened or disturbed. Nor did he seem to make any effort to hold his horses in. Billy stared into the cloud of dust which followed him. What did it mean? And as he stared the horses stopped, skillfully drawn in by Jakie Barsinger's firm hand beside the yellow platform. The cloud of dust thinned a little, and Billy saw plainly now. Into the front seat of the tourists' carriage, beside Jakie Barsinger, climbed the President of the United States. Billy rose in his seat.

"Colonel Mott!" he called, frantically. "Colonel Mott!"

But no one heeded. If any one heard, he thought it was but another cheer. The crowd swarmed down to the road shouting, huzzaing, here and there a man or a girl pausing to steady a camera on a fence-post, here and there a father lifting his child to his shoulder.

"Where is the President?" they asked, and Billy heard the answer.

"There, there! Look! By Jakie Barsinger!"

The old man's hands dropped, and he sobbed. It had all been so neatly done: the pretense of a runaway, the confusion of the moment, Colonel Mott's excitement — and the crown of his life was gone.

Long after the crowd had followed in the dusty wake of Jakie Barsinger's carriage, he turned his horses toward home. A hundred tourists had begged him to take them over the field, but he had silently shaken his head. He could not speak. Dan and Bess trotted briskly, mindful of the cool stable toward which their heads were set, and they whinnied eagerly at the stable door. They stood there for half an hour, however, before their master clambered down to unharness them. He talked to himself feebly, and, when he had finished, went out, not to the house, where Abbie, who had watched Jakie Barsinger drive by, waited in an agony of fear, but down the street, and out by quiet alleys and lanes to the National Cemetery. Sometimes he looked a little wonderingly toward the crowded main streets, not able to recall instantly why the crowd was there, then remembering with a rage which shook him to the soul. Fleeting, futile suggestions of revenge rushed upon him — a loosened nut in Jakie Barsinger's swingle-tree or a cut trace — and were repelled with horror which hurt as much as the rage. All the town would taunt him now. Why had he not turned his carriage across the road and stopped Jakie Barsinger in his wild dash? It would have been better to have been killed than to have lived to this.

Around the gate of the cemetery a company of cavalry was stationed, and within new thousands of visitors waited. It was afternoon now, and almost time for the trip over the field to end and the exercises to begin. As Billy passed through the crowd, he felt a hand on his shoulder.

"Thought you were going to drive the President," said a loud voice.

Billy saw for an instant the strange faces about him, gaping, interested to hear his answer.

"I ain't nobody's coachman," he said coolly, and walked on.

"They ain't goin' to get a rise out of me," he choked. "They ain't goin' to get a rise out of me."

He walked slowly up the wide avenue, and presently sat down on a bench. He was tired to death, his head nodded, and soon he slept, regardless of blare of band and shouting of men and roll of carriage wheels. There was a song, and then a prayer, but Billy heard nothing until the great speech was almost over. Then he opened his eyes drowsily, and saw the throng gathered round the wistaria-covered rostrum, on which the President was standing. Billy sprang up. At least he would hear the speech. Nobody could cheat him out of that. He pushed his way through the crowd, which, seeing his white hair, opened easily enough. Then he stood trembling, all his misery rushing over him again at sight of the tall figure. He was to have sat beside him, to have talked with him! He rubbed a weak hand across his eyes. Suddenly he realized that the formal portion of the speech was over, the President was saying now a short farewell.

"I wish to congratulate the Commission which has made of this great field so worthy a memorial to those who died here. I wish to express my gratification to the citizens of this town for their share in the preservation of the field, and their extraordinary knowledge of the complicated tactics of the battle. Years ago my interest was aroused by hearing my father tell of a visit here, and of the vivid story of a guide — his name, I think, was William Gude. I —"

"'His name, I think,'" old Billy repeated dully. "'His name, I think, was William Gude.'"

It was a few seconds before the purport of

it reached his brain. Then he raised both arms, unaware that the speech was ended and that the crowd had begun to cheer.

"Oh, Mr. President," he called, "my name is William Gude!" His head swam. They were turning away; they did not hear. "My name is William Gude," he said again pitifully.

The crowd, pressing toward Jakie Barsinger's carriage, into which the President was stepping, carried him with them. They looked about them questioningly; they could see Colonel Mott, who was at the President's side, beckoning to some one; who it was they could not tell. Then above the noise they heard him call.

"Billy Gude!" he shouted. "Billy —"

"It's me!" said Billy.

He stared, blinking, at Colonel Mott and at the President.

Colonel Mott laid his hand on Billy's shoulder. He had been trying to invent a suitable punishment for Jakie Barsinger. No more custom should come to him through the Commission.

"The President wants you to ride down to the station with him, Billy," he said. "He wants to know whether you remember his father."

As in a dream, Billy climbed into the carriage. The President sat on the rear seat now, and Billy was beside him.

"I remember him like yesterday," he declared. "I remember what he said an' how he looked, an'—" the words crowded upon each other as eagerly as the President's questions, and Billy forgot all save them — the cheering crowd, the wondering, envious eyes of his fellow citizens; he did not even remember that Jakie Barsinger was driving him, Billy Gude, and the President of the United States together. Once he caught a glimpse of Abbie's frightened face, and he waved his hand and the President lifted his hat.

"I wish I could have known about you earlier in the day," said the President, as he stepped down at the railroad station. Then he took Billy's hand in his. "It has been a great pleasure to talk to you."

The engine puffed near at hand, there

were new cheers from throats already hoarse with cheering, and the great man was gone, the great day over. For an instant Billy watched the train, his hand uplifted with a thousand other hands in a last salute to the swift-vanishing figure in the observation-car. Then he turned, to meet the unwilling eyes of Jakie Barsinger, helpless to move his carriage in the great crowd. For an instant the recollection of his wrongs overwhelmed him.

"Jakie —" he began. Then he laughed. The crowd was listening, open-mouthed. For the moment, now that the President was gone, he, Billy Gude, was the great man. He stepped nimbly into the carriage. "Coachman," he commanded, "you can drive home."

IX
MARY BOWMAN

IX

MARY BOWMAN

OUTSIDE the broad gateway which leads into the National Cemetery at Gettysburg and thence on into the great park, there stands a little house on whose porch there may be seen on summer evenings an old woman. The cemetery with its tall monuments lies a little back of her and to her left; before her is the village; beyond, on a little eminence, the buildings of the Theological Seminary; and still farther beyond the foothills of the Blue Ridge. The village is tree-shaded, the hills are set with fine oaks and hickories, the fields are green. It would be difficult to find in all the world an expanse more lovely. Those who have known it in their youth grow homesick for it; their eyes ache and their throats tighten as they remember it. At sunset it is bathed in purple light, its trees grow darker, its hills more shadowy,

its hollows deeper and more mysterious.
Then, lifted above the dark masses of the
trees, one may see marble shafts and domes
turn to liquid gold.

The little old woman, sitting with folded
hands, is Mary Bowman, whose husband was
lost on this field. The battle will soon be fifty
years in the past, she has been for that long
a widow. She has brought up three children,
two sons and a daughter. One of her sons is
a merchant, one is a clergyman, and her daughter is well and happily married. Her own life
of activity is past; she is waited upon tenderly
and loved dearly by her children and her
grandchildren. She was born in this village,
she has almost never been away. From here
her husband went to war, here he is buried
among thousands of unknown dead, here she
nursed the wounded and dying, here she will
be buried herself in the Evergreen cemetery,
beyond the National cemetery.

She has seen beauty change to desolation,
trees shattered, fields trampled, walls broken,
all her dear, familiar world turned to chaos;
she has seen desolation grow again to beauty.

These hills and streams were always lovely,
now a nation has determined to keep them
forever in the same loveliness. Here was a
rocky, wooded field, destined by its owner to
cultivation; it has been decreed that its rough
picturesqueness shall endure forever. Here is
a lowly farmhouse; upon it no hand of change
shall be laid while the nation continues. Preserved, consecrated, hallowed are the woods
and lanes in which Mary Bowman walked
with the lover of her youth.

Broad avenues lead across the fields, mark-
ing the lines where by thousands Northerners
and Southerners were killed. Big Round Top,
to which one used to journey by a difficult
path, is now accessible; Union and Confederate soldiers, returning, find their way with
ease to old positions; lads from West Point are
brought to see, spread out before them as on a
map, that Union fish-hook, five miles long, in-
closing that slightly curved Confederate line.

Monuments are here by hundreds, names
by thousands, cast in bronze, as endurable
as they can be made by man. All that can be
done in remembrance of those who fought

here has been done, all possible effort to identify the unknown has been made. For fifty years their little trinkets have been preserved, their pocket Testaments, their photographs, their letters — letters addressed to "My precious son," "My dear brother," "My beloved husband." Seeing them to-day, you will find them marked by a number. This stained scapular, this little housewife with its rusty scissors, this unsigned letter, dated in '63, belonged to him who lies now in Grave Number 20 or Number 3500.

There is almost an excess of tenderness for these dead, yet mixed with it is a strange feeling of remoteness. We mourn them, praise them, laud them, but we cannot understand them. To this generation war is strange, its sacrifices are uncomprehended, incomprehensible. It is especially so in these latter years, since those who came once to this field come now no more. Once the heroes of the war were familiar figures upon these streets; Meade with his serious, bearded face, Slocum with his quick, glancing eyes, Hancock with his distinguished air, Howard with his empty sleeve. They have gone hence, and with them have marched two thirds of Gettysburg's two hundred thousand.

Mary Bowman has seen them all, has heard them speak. Sitting on her little porch, she has watched most of the great men of the United States go by, Presidents, cabinet officials, ambassadors, army officers, and also famous visitors from other lands who know little of the United States, but to whom Gettysburg is as a familiar country. She has watched also that great, rapidly shrinking army of private soldiers in faded blue coats, who make pilgrimages to see the fields and hills upon which they fought. She has tried to make herself realize that her husband, if he had lived, would be like these old men, maimed, feeble, decrepit, but the thought possesses no reality for her. He is still young, still erect, he still goes forth in the pride of life and strength.

Mary Bowman will not talk about the battle. To each of her children and each of her grandchildren, she has told once, as one who performs a sacred duty, its many-sided story.

She has told each one of wounds and suffering, but she has not omitted tales of heroic death, of promotion on the field, of stubborn fight for glory. By others than her own she will not be questioned. A young officer, recounting the rigors of the march, has written, "Forsan et hæc olim meminisse juvabit,"—"Perchance even these things it will be delightful to remember." To feel delight, remembering these things, Mary Bowman has never learned. Her neighbors who suffered with her, some just as cruelly, have recovered; their wounds have healed, as wounds do in the natural course of things. But Mary Bowman has remained mindful; she has been, for all these years, widowed indeed.

Her faithful friend and neighbor, Hannah Casey, is the great joy of visitors to the battlefield. She will talk incessantly, enthusiastically, with insane invention. The most morbid visitor will be satisfied with Hannah's wild account of a Valley of Death filled to the rim with dead bodies, of the trickling rivulet of Plum Creek swollen with blood to a roaring torrent. But Mary Bowman is different.

Her granddaughter, who lives with her, is curious about her emotions.

"Do you feel reconciled?" she will ask. "Do you feel reconciled to the sacrifice, grandmother? Do you think of the North and South as reunited, and are you glad you helped?"

Her grandmother answers with no words, but with a slow, tearful smile. She does not analyze her emotions. Perhaps it is too much to expect of one who has been a widow for fifty years, that she philosophize about it!

Sitting on her porch in the early morning, she remembers the first of July, fifty years ago.

"Madam!" cried the soldier who galloped to the door, "there is to be a battle in this town!"

"Here?" she had answered stupidly. "*Here?*"

Sitting there at noon, she hears the roaring blasts of artillery, she seems to see shells, as of old, curving like great ropes through the air, she remembers that somewhere on this field, struck by a missile such as that, her husband fell.

Sitting there in the moonlight, she remembers Early on his white horse, with muffled hoofs, riding spectralwise down the street among the sleeping soldiers.

"Up, boys!" he whispers, and is heard even in that heavy stupor. "Up, boys, up! We must get away!"

She hears also the pouring rain of July the fourth, falling upon her little house, upon that wide battle-field, upon her very heart. She sees, too, the deep, sad eyes of Abraham Lincoln, she hears his voice in the great sentences of his simple speech, she feels his message in her soul.

"Daughter!" he seems to say, "Daughter, be of good comfort!"

So, still, Mary Bowman sits waiting. She is a Christian, she has great hope; as her waiting has been long, so may the joy of her reunion be full.

THE END

CLASSICS OF CIVIL WAR FICTION

DAVID RACHELS AND DAVID MADDEN, *Series Editors*

The Battle-Ground by Ellen Glasgow
Introduction by Susan Goodman

Manassas: A Novel of the War by Upton Sinclair
Introduction by Kent Gramm

*Andersonville Violets: A Story of Northern and Southern
Life* by Herbert W. Collingwood
Introduction by David Rachels and Robert Baird

Cudjo's Cave by J. T. Trowbridge
Introduction by Dean Rehberger

Gettysburg: Stories of Memory, Grief, and Greatness
Introduction by Lesley J. Gordon